PRAISE FOR KIM PAFFEN

DYING TO LIVE
a novel of life among the undead

"*Dying to Live* is not just a thinking man's horror novel, it's a zombie book for philosophers. There's plenty of action—and we enter the story while it's already in gear—and we get inside the head and heart of a moral man trying to understand the cosmic implications of the apocalypse."

—Jonathan Maberry, author of *Ghost Road Blues*

"Kim Paffenroth put me on the edge of my seat from the opening scene of this apocalyptic thriller and never let up. His prose is gritty and tough, as horrific and as multilayered as a Brueghel painting, but it is always intelligent, always with something insightful to say about the human condition. *Dying to Live* is a truly powerful achievement. Don't miss it."

—Joe McKinney, author of *Dead City*

"Kim Paffenroth writes with passion, bringing a human element to a world of the inhuman. His love of the zombie genre is matched only by his insight in posing philosophical questions of those surviving the apocalypse. Intelligent and never boring, *Dying to Live* is as good as the zombie genre gets."

—Scott A. Johnson, author of *Deadlands*

"A grave new world . . . a startlingly original vision of the direction of the whole human race. . . . This is as bloody, violent and intense as it gets. An intelligent novel that will make you think and make you squirm with disgust in equal measure."

—David Moody, author of the *Autumn* series

Dying to Live

a novel of life among the undead

Kim Paffenroth

Gallery Books
New York London Toronto Sydney

Gallery Books
A Division of Simon & Schuster, Inc.
1230 Avenue of the Americas
New York, NY 10020

This book is a work of fiction. Names, characters, places, and incidents either are products of the author's imagination or are used fictitiously. Any resemblance to actual events or locales or persons, living or dead, is entirely coincidental.

Originally published in 2006 by Permuted Press.

First Gallery Books trade paperback edition September 2010

GALLERY BOOKS and colophon are trademarks of Simon & Schuster, Inc.

For information about special discounts for bulk purchases, please contact Simon & Schuster Special Sales at 1-866-506-1949 or business@simonandschuster.com.

The Simon & Schuster Speakers Bureau can bring authors to your live event. For more information or to book an event contact the Simon & Schuster Speakers Bureau at 1-866-248-3049 or visit our website at www.simonspeakers.com.

Manufactured in the United States of America

10 9 8 7 6 5 4 3 2 1

ISBN 978-1-4391-8071-6
ISBN 978-1-4391-8074-7 (ebook)

Dedicated to St. Augustine
and George A. Romero—
two of the greatest philosophers
of the dark side of human nature

O death, where is thy victory?

1 Corinthians 15:55

To sue to live, I find I seek to die,
And seeking death, find life. Let it come on.

Shakespeare, *Measure for Measure* 3.1.42–43

Chapter One

I AWOKE TO find a lone zombie underneath my little hideaway. The tree house I had spent the night in was poorly constructed—the bottom was just a square of plywood, reinforced with a couple boards, with plywood walls on three sides and the fourth one open. It had no roof, but the sky was clear, so no bother. All the pieces were irregular and unpainted, with big gaps between them in many spots, and the walls were only between two and three feet high. But it was higher up than most, a good twelve feet off the ground (the kid's mom must've been one of the ones we always called a "cool mom," to allow such a dangerous playhouse), so I was even more surprised to see my unwanted visitor.

I scanned the surrounding field and trees and saw that the zombie and I were alone; my heart slowed down. In a few moments, my situation had gone from peaceful morning reverie, to possible or near-certain death, to minor inconvenience. In that respect, this was a typical morning.

Tree houses, and any other little platform above the ground, were my favorite places to catch a couple hours of sleep at night as I made my way across the country. Going inside a building required a careful search, and later on, as you tried to sleep, you'd

start to worry that maybe you had missed some hiding place, from which the real Boogie Man, who doesn't need sleep, would rise up during the night. And building the necessary barricades on the doors and windows often made so much noise you could end up with a growing crowd of the undead, whose moaning and clawing at the doors would probably keep you up, on top of the danger they would pose when you tried to leave your shelter in the morning. Unless you were in a group, a building was not a good choice for your little motel in hell.

Little platforms above ground, on the other hand, were ideal. Not comfortable, but ideal. You usually had to lash yourself to them so you wouldn't fall off in the night, and you almost always had to sleep sitting up, but that was nothing for a few blessed hours of relative peace of mind. The undead are by nature incurious and almost never look up, so the chances of being spotted once you were in your little eyrie were low. For exactly the same reason that hunters once used them, back when humans were the hunters rather than the hunted, your scent wouldn't usually carry down to the creatures below, either. The tree houses always made me a little sad, 'cause they reminded me of my kids, but what could you do? All in all, my little sky boxes were the best places I had found to spend the night, so long as the living dead were afoot. But best, of course, had never been the same as perfect, and that was infinitely more true now.

One reason the zombie and I were alone this morning was that it lacked the ability to make sound. Like so many of its kind, its throat was torn open, leaving its windpipe a ragged hole, and the front of its suit stained brown with blood.

It looked up at me with its listless, cloudy eyes that lacked all expression—not hatred, not evil, not even hunger, just

blanks. It was chilling in its own way, like the stare of a snake or an insect. Its look would never change, whether you drove a spike through its head, or it sank its yellow teeth into your soft, warm flesh; it lacked all capacity to be afraid, or to be satisfied. Its mouth, however, had a great deal more bestial expression to it, for it was wide open, almost gnawing at the bark of the tree as it clawed upward.

I stood looking down at it for a few moments. It was times like this—and there had been several in the last few months—that I had always wished that I smoked. In a few seconds, I would fight this thing and one or both of us would cease to exist—"die" is obviously the wrong word here—and just to stand here and contemplate that inevitability cried out for some distraction, some mindless and sensual habit like smoking, to make it less horrible. I guess I could've chewed gum, but that would make the whole scene ridiculous, when it was really as serious, overwhelming, and sad as any that had ever occurred to a man.

With nothing to distract me, I just felt the full weight of a terrible and necessary task, and the tediousness and unfairness of it. I had just awakened from a relatively peaceful sleep, and I already felt a crushing weariness coming over me. Again, it was developing into a pretty typical morning.

People had come up with lots of names for the walking dead in the preceding months. While we weren't fighting them off or running like hell, we usually came up with humorous labels. "Meat puppets" was a popular one. Somebody came up with "Jacks and Janes," like they were just some annoying neighbors from the next circle of hell, or as a variation on "Jack-offs."

Sometimes, when they'd get especially noisy and rambunctious, but didn't pose any immediate threat, we'd call them "the natives," as in "the natives are restless." Maybe that was a little racist, I don't know. "Walking stiffs" was pretty accurate. But mostly we'd go for the tried and true—zombies. That's what they were, and we'd always be one breath away from becoming one—a mindless, shambling bag of flesh.

My zombie this morning looked to have been a middle-aged man in its human life, slightly graying, average build. Its suit was intact, and other than its throat wound, there were no signs of further fights with humans or other zombies. Decay had taken its toll, and it looked more desiccated than gooey, a brittle husk rather than the dripping bag of pus that some of them became.

At first, I looked it over to size up its threat and plan my attack, but that quickly turned into contemplating its human existence. Maybe his kids had built the tree house, and that's why he'd been hanging around here, almost as if he were protecting it, or waiting for them to come back. Or even worse, maybe his kids had been the ones to tear out his throat, when he had rushed home in the midst of the outbreak, hoping against hope they were still okay. Or, just as bad, maybe he'd been bitten at work or on the way home, only to break in to his own house and kill his kids.

My mind reeled, and I clutched the wall of the tree house. I'd heard of soldiers in other wars having a "thousand yard stare," a blank look that signaled they were giving in to the hopelessness and horror around them, soon to be dead or insane. As for me, I was suffering the thousand yard stare of the war with the undead: once you contemplated the zombies as human beings, once you thought of them as having kids and lives and loves and worries and hopes and fears, you might as well just put your gun in your mouth and be done with it right

then, because you were losing it—fast. But, God knows, if you never looked at them that way, if they were just meat puppets whose heads exploded in your rifle's sights, then hopefully somebody would put a bullet in your brain, because you had become more monstrous than any zombie ever could be.

I shook myself free of my paralysis. I'm not exactly sure why, but I wasn't ready to give up yet. I tossed my backpack beyond where the zombie stood. It turned to see where it landed, then immediately looked back up at me. Its head lolled from side to side, and I was again glad that it couldn't vocalize, as it was clearly getting worked up and would've been making quite a racket if it could.

You never used a gun if you didn't have to, for its noise brought lots of unwanted attention, so I pulled out a knife, the one I carried with a long, thin blade, like a bayonet, as that would work best. I stood at the edge of the plywood platform. "I'm sorry," I said, looking right in the zombie's eyes. "Maybe somewhere, deep down, you still understand: I'm sorry."

I took a step forward and started to fall. I tried to hit it on the shoulder with my right foot, but its arms were flailing about, and my boot hit its left wrist, sliding along its arm. I sprawled to the right and then rolled away as the zombie was shoved into the tree.

As it turned to face me, I scrambled up, took a step forward, and drove the knife into its left eye. Its hands flailed about, either to attack me or to ward off the blow. The blade was long and thin enough that it went almost to the back of its skull. The whole attack was noiseless, without so much as the sound of a squish or a glitch as the blade slid through its eyeball and brain.

As I drew the blade out, I grabbed the zombie by the hair

and shoved it downward to the side, where it fell to the ground and lay motionless.

And that was that. Like everyone, I always used to imagine deadly fights would be much more dramatic. But in my experience, there were seldom any Chuck Norris flying, spinning kicks, or any *Matrix*-style running up the wall while firing two guns on full auto. If anyone's ever around to make movies about the wars against the undead, maybe there will be such moves in them, I don't know. But usually, like this morning, there were just a couple of savage, clumsy blows, and it was over.

I was barely breathing at all, let alone breathing hard, the way I felt someone should when they kill something that was somehow, in some small way, still human. A few months ago, I would've at least felt nauseous, but not anymore. Looking down at the creature from the tree house had been much more traumatic than delivering the killing blow.

I bent down over my would-be killer and cleaned the blade on his suit jacket. I then reached into his pocket. It was a little ritual I still followed when I could, though the horrible exigencies of a zombie-infested world usually made it impossible. I pulled out his wallet and got out his driver's license. Rather than look at the bloody horror at my feet, with its one undead eye and one bloody, vacant socket, I stared at his driver's license picture—smiling, happy, alive, years and decades of life ahead of him. I cleared my throat to speak clearly. "I have killed Daniel Gerard. I hope he's somewhere better now."

I cast the wallet and license on top of his motionless body, scooped up my backpack, and hurried away.

It had been close to a year since all the worst parts of the Bible started coming true. Armageddon. Apocalypse. The End of Days. God's righteous judgment on a sinful humanity. Whatever the self-righteous jerk who railed at you once a week from a pulpit used to call it. Well, he might have been self-righteous and a jerk, and now he was probably lurching around like most everyone else, drooling on himself with half his face torn off, but it sure seemed as though he had had some inside information that we all wish we'd gotten a little sooner.

For most people, I assume it started like every other day. Brush your teeth. Kiss your spouse without any feeling. Go to work. Grab whatever it is you grab to eat on your way to work. Eat it, not really noticing or enjoying it. But then at some point that blessed, kind, comforting routine goes horribly awry and someone—maybe your neighbor, or coworker, or worse, your kids or your spouse—staggers up to you with a blank look and tries to tear your throat out with his teeth. If he gets you, then you don't have to worry anymore, because you'll be dead, and then you'll get up and wander around like him, with no more thoughts or feelings, just shuffling around trying to bite people. If you get away from him, then you'd be one of the survivors, at least for a little while, and then you'd have lots of worries, and your only feeling would be fear. Either way—welcome to hell.

Theological assessments aside, the automatic assumption was that the dead were rising and killing because of some infection, and the infection was spread by their bites. The next logical assumption—since there was not much reliable evidence of zombie infestations before the 21st century (horror movies notwithstanding)—was that we had tinkered with viruses and DNA and had brought all this shit on ourselves.

Here again, a theological assessment was hard to avoid. We had created a hell on earth through our own arrogance and ignorance, and now we were reaping what we had sown—with a vengeance. Worse than any couple who ate an apple or any bozo who slapped some brick and mortar on the Tower of Babel, we'd messed with The Man's prerogatives, and either He'd given us the biggest damn smack down of all time, or we'd just set off something that only He could control. Shit, you didn't need to believe in the Bible to see how much sense it made. You remember that crazy Greek myth you read about in fifth grade—Pandora's box. Same damn thing. A box full of walking cannibal corpses who wouldn't let you close it once it got open.

Now, how that box got opened, that was a hot topic of debate among survivors, when we weren't fighting to prolong our miserable existence and could afford the luxury of conversation or discussion. Outright warfare or a terrorist attack was probably the least popular theory, though it had vigorous proponents. I don't know why more of us didn't subscribe to that hypothesis. I suppose it's funny to say, but I think we didn't because it was the least comforting of all our speculations. It was too horrible to imagine that even terrorists could unleash the hellish plague of undeath on the whole world, even their own people, including women, children, and the elderly. And at the same time, the theory made it too pat and simple, like it was just some crazies who did this, some tiny band of malcontents—horror of this magnitude seemed to require a more powerful, far-reaching source.

That's probably why more people bought into the paranoid, conspiratorial theory that the disease had been released by our government or someone else's as a horribly botched attempt to test it on a real population. Proponents of this theory almost delighted in its vindication of every real and imagined form of government-sponsored terror, from Andersonville to Tuskegee to Gitmo to putting fluoride in the tap water. Their tales could almost be the bedtime stories of the apocalypse, lulling us to sleep with some tiny and bizarre shred of hope that even now, the world made some weird kind of sense, that undeath was not a new and incomprehensible kind of evil, but just a continuation of this world's madness and brutality, like Jackie scrambling on the trunk of the Lincoln to grab the big chunk of her husband's head that was sliding around back there, or like bulldozers pushing mountains of emaciated bodies into pits in Dachau. Strange comfort, that, but it was often all we had.

But the most popular theory—the one I personally advocated, though without much conviction—was simply that there had been a horrible accident. Nothing malevolent or calculated, just plain old human error. Somebody dropped a test tube somewhere. A lab monkey bit through somebody's glove. The kind of thing that happens a thousand times a day for thousands of days with no fatal outcome. It was the most blackly humorous theory, I suppose, for it made the misery and violent deaths of billions of people just the result of a stupid mistake, but it had its own cold comfort. If all this was just some blunder, then maybe, if we could ever shoot every zombie in the head—the only way we had found to kill them permanently—or if they would just eventually rot and fall apart—what everyone had hoped for initially—then we could go back to life like it used to be. We weren't evil, just stupid and clumsy. Like poor Pandora.

That's how some of us theorized that it had begun. But

whatever had happened—and I've left out the more exotic theories, like an extra-terrestrial source of infection—we ended up in the same place. Almost one year after the first corpse rose, the world was ruled by the undead, who wandered about with no discernible goal other than to kill and eat living people. The undead were everywhere, the new dominant species that took the place of the old, extinct one. Places where there had been large human populations were especially thick with the walking dead, though they never took any notice of one another.

The living, meanwhile, as was their wont, almost always congregated in little groups. The government or society or culture had imploded or disintegrated with terrifying speed as the infection spread. Within hours, there had been no telephone service, no police or rescue response to the terrified calls for help. Within days, there was no power or television. And within weeks, the last organized military and government resistance collapsed, at least in the U.S.

But groups of survivors quickly came together into little groups, little communities with a pecking order and rules and authority, but also some of the little perks of being around other people—companionship, conversation, sex, someone to hold your hand when you die, someone to put a bullet in your brain when you went to get back up as a zombie. (And if you've ever seen a zombie—and God love you, I hope you haven't, but if you're reading this, I suspect you have—then you know that last perk is by no means the least important one.) You didn't have to be a damned philosopher to know that we're social animals, and would be till the last zombie bit the last human and dragged us all down to hell, which, judging by the zombies, looked like it was going to be the most unsociable place imaginable.

Yes, humans always build their little communities in order to survive, and in order to make surviving a little more bearable. Except me. I was alone. And it sucked. It was dangerous and it sucked.

By midday, I was moving closer to what looked like a small-sized city. I had thrown my maps away a few days ago when I had failed to find my family. After that, I figured, I didn't have much need for maps: if I didn't have any place to go anymore—and I had decided that I didn't—what difference did it make where I was at the moment? Besides, the end of civilization had wreaked a lot of havoc with the things depicted on maps: I guess the rivers and mountains were still there, but cities were gone, roads were clogged with wrecked cars, bridges and tunnels and dams had been blown up to try to stop the rampaging hordes of the undead. So long as I was out of reach of those things, and had one bullet for myself if it came to that, I was in about the best location I could hope for.

It was a late spring day, bursting with a sunshine that didn't make it hot, but just made things seem better, brighter, more alive than they were on other days. I still had the instinct to call it beautiful as I looked around and forgot the obvious shortcomings of the day for a moment. One shortcoming I couldn't forget, however, was the gnawing hunger I felt.

Never one for breakfast, I had definitely been put off from eating anything this morning after killing Daniel Gerard, a man who, after all, had only been looking for something to eat, just as I was. I had some supplies in my backpack, but if I was

near an area where I could forage for more and conserve what I had, that would be the much wiser course.

The undead weren't exactly afraid of sunlight—they weren't afraid of anything—but they did seem to avoid it unless aroused and provoked. Maybe it hurt their skin or eyes, or maybe they could sense that it was speeding their decay and that brought them some discomfort. Whatever it was, during bright daylight, you could walk through places where the walking dead were nearby without immediately attracting a crowd, so long as you were quiet and downwind. Still, I never went too far into an urban area. Right now, I just wanted to find some food and get back out to the sticks before nightfall.

From what I'd seen, many cities had burned more or less to the ground, once fire crews were no longer there to put out the inevitable fires. But here, for whatever reason of wind or rain or luck, many buildings were still standing. Some were gutted or damaged by fire, and all had the usual marks of looting, ransacking, and the final, desperate battles between the living and the dead. There were few unbroken windows.

In the street, wrecked or abandoned cars were everywhere. There were a few bodies and pieces of bodies in extremely advanced stages of decay, and paper and dead leaves rustled about on a light breeze.

The sight of the burnt-out remains of a city was almost as overwhelmingly depressing as the human wrecks that wandered everywhere as zombies: this place should be bustling and alive, and instead it was—quite literally—a graveyard.

I always wondered why there weren't more animals around now, since zombies didn't eat them, but everywhere I went, it always seemed like there were even fewer animals than when people had ruled the earth. I almost never heard a bird sing. I

seldom saw pigeons or squirrels. It was almost as though even the animals fled from such horror, fled when the ruler of the animal kingdom died, and left the king's mausoleum in peace, until it could completely crumble away and they could reclaim it after a suitable mourning period. I know it seems almost delusional in its anthropomorphism, but sometimes you can't help thinking like that when you're alone in these dead places.

I checked the remains of a couple stores, barely venturing inside the darkened buildings, for fear of the dead hiding in ambush. The inventories of a clothing store and a jewelry store were barely touched: it was funny how quickly things had been re-prioritized in the final, chaotic days of the human race.

I looked at what appeared to be hundreds of thousands of dollars of diamonds, now mixed in with the smashed glass of the cases that had once displayed them: both sparkled in the sun, but their value had been radically and traumatically equalized a few months ago. I imagined that during last winter—the first winter of a world that would now remain more or less dead in every season—the snow too had sparkled just as brightly when it blew in and covered the diamonds that, in better times, would've adorned hundreds of brides.

A quick look into a liquor store revealed much less remaining stock—human nature and appetites being what they are—but there was a bottle of some bad bourbon just a few feet inside the door, so I reached in and grabbed it. I didn't know when I'd be able to drop my guard enough to partake, but since I wasn't carrying that much, it made sense to take it.

I knew I was getting too far into the dead city, but on the next street was a convenience store where there might be food. It was facing perpendicularly from the stores I had examined, so at least it would be brighter inside. The big front windows

were still intact, but the glass of the front door had been smashed. Looking up and down the street and still seeing no movement, I went inside.

I was looking for snack cakes. When the final crisis of humanity had begun, people had instinctively stocked up on canned food: I guess Spam is forever etched in our collective consciousness as the foodstuff of the apocalypse. People at first had bought up everything canned, and then, within just a couple days, as cash became utterly worthless and stores weren't even open, the stronger smashed and grabbed from the weaker. I had never seen a can of food in a store since I had started foraging: you could only find cans in people's houses, and even then they were getting pretty rare at this point. So, for now, snack cakes were the way to go. What I would do when those finally went bad and the last few cans ran out—that was a question still a few months off, and therefore way beyond any reasonable contingency plans.

I don't know if all the old urban legends that Twinkies and those pink Snow Ball cakes could survive a nuclear explosion were true, but they and their kind definitely had a shelf life well over a year, if the box wasn't opened and you weren't fussy, which I clearly wasn't at this point.

There was a treasure trove of them in the second aisle into the store, and I smiled when I saw there were no chocolate ones: I guessed some priorities remained effective right up till the last gasp of humanity. I made my way quietly to them, tore open the boxes, shoveled a bunch of the wrapped ones into my backpack, and proceeded to gorge myself on what I couldn't carry. I was licking white crème filling off my fingers when I heard the crunch of a shoe stepping on broken glass.

Chapter Two

THE ZOMBIE WAS about twelve feet away from me, at the end of the Twinkie aisle. It was staggering toward me with the usual slow, stiff motions of the undead. It had been a teenage girl, blonde and pretty, as far as I could tell now, wearing her boyfriend's high school letter jacket, way too big for her. Its mouth moved noiselessly, except for the clacking of her bloody, yellow teeth.

The jacket was open, and the lower half of her t-shirt was flayed and soaked with blood, which also had soaked her jeans down past her knees. Her abdomen was torn wide open in a wound about a foot wide. They'd ripped all her organs out when they killed her. She wasn't moaning now the way zombies usually did, because she didn't have lungs. You could see right through to her ribs and spine, not glistening and drippy the way a wound on a living person would be, but dark and dry and caked, like mummies I'd seen in museums.

It was coming closer, slowly but inexorably, but I couldn't look away from that horrible tribute to mortality and incarnation. You saw all kinds of wounds on the living dead, but some still commanded shock, almost a reverential awe at the miracle of life and the horrible mystery of death. Partly you were aghast at the

perverse will to go on "living," despite terrible mutilation and decay: why couldn't it just lie down and die? Just rest, damn it, and stop struggling. Ashes to ashes, dust to dust—that was how it was supposed to be, and this was some hideous violation of nature.

But mostly, you couldn't help the pity that spasmed up from your own gut, putting a lump in your throat, at how awful and degrading and unfair the person's death must have been. People—even young and pretty ones—died in car crashes, or from diseases, or in war, or from horrible crimes, and their young, healthy bodies might even be mutilated and disfigured. Such deaths were hard enough to take without anger and despair. But no one was supposed to be gutted like a fish, butchered like an animal, and left to dry out like a damn piece of jerky. You might see shit go down most every day, but if you were going to go on living, you had to know, deep down, that some things were still just plain wrong, and you could still let out a primal scream against them as some kind of evil abomination. And what I was staring at in that convenience store, on a glorious spring day, licking sweet white crème off my fingers, was as wrong as anything ever could be.

There was that damn thousand yard stare again, closing me off, tunneling my vision and lulling me to just let go.

To my left, something roared, and I turned. Over the shelves, which were about at chin level, like they usually were in convenience stores, I could see what could only be described as a hairless bear, its arms out in front, Frankenstein-like, lurching toward me. I swear the thing looked like it had been a professional wrestler in its human life—probably 350 pounds, almost a head taller than me, covered in tattoos, though its flesh was now a mottled gray that obscured much of the artwork.

It crashed into the shelves, tipping them over onto me and the other zombie. I was pushed back and pinned against the opposite shelves as the monster scrabbled at my face with its foul nails; the shelving unit kept it from getting closer. The girl zombie wasn't pinned as tightly as I was, so she was still slowly working her way toward me, teeth clacking.

The top shelf was pressing into my upper chest and arms, making it hard to breathe, as well as almost impossible to get to a weapon, and even if I did, I wouldn't be able to bring it up to eye level to get a head shot at either of them. I had no leverage to push the shelving unit off me, and I wasn't sure I could do it anyway, as the zombie was so much bigger than me.

I struggled and drew my .357 magnum from the holster in the small of my back. I'd have to shoot from the hip. I fired, and my ears started ringing from the roar of the magnum. The plate glass window behind the big zombie shattered as the bullet went through his torso. A bullet anywhere other than through the brain won't put a zombie down, but this one made it stagger back just enough for me to push the shelving unit off of me.

The zombie lunged again—I stuck the barrel in its face and fired. Its arms shot up as it spun around and dropped on its face, the back of its head blown off.

I turned as the girl zombie grabbed my shoulder. This was it. Another second and she'd sink her teeth into me—then it wouldn't really matter if I shot her or not: the bite would kill me and turn me into a zombie in a matter of hours or days.

I grabbed her hair, wrenched myself free from her grip, and shoved the barrel of the gun under her chin. I yanked her head down and to the left, so she wasn't looking at me. "I'm sorry," I rasped as I pulled the trigger. Her brains were blasted out in a gray slop all over the ceiling surveillance camera and the cigarette display case above the counter.

I shoved her away from me, and she fell on her back with a cracking sound. I was panting and drenched in sweat. I grabbed my backpack and looked down at her one more time. Thankfully, her long hair covered her face. I pulled the flap of the too-large jacket across her belly. What a world, where that'd be considered an unusually kind gesture, covering up the magnificent corpse I had made out of what had been a ninety-five pound girl.

As I stood up, I heard the moaning underneath the ringing in my ears, and I suddenly felt icy cold. One zombie was already stepping through the broken window. At least ten were closing in on the shattered storefront, and I knew there were dozens more nearby, and hundreds more behind them.

It was getting seriously close to being time for me to eat a bullet. At least then I might get to see God and ask Him what all this shit had been about. Some days, like the days when I blew a teenager's brains all over the ceiling, I wouldn't even mind meeting the *other* guy. At least with Old Nick, it seemed like you knew better where you stood.

I made my way to the back exit of the store, holstering the magnum, shouldering my backpack, and drawing my Glock. The magnum was wild overkill against zombies anyway, and with three of its six shots fired and no time to reload, the seventeen-round magazine of the 9mm would increase what little chance I had.

I was only a few steps ahead of the growing horde of

zombies filling the store. If I couldn't get the back door open, or if there were more outside when I opened it, it was all over. You couldn't risk a close-in fight with them: they might grab your gun arm and make it impossible to shoot yourself.

The closest zombie was at the end of the hallway that led to the backdoor, maybe fifteen feet away from me. Several were right behind it, and more were shuffling in steadily—old women in housecoats, men in suits, young people in shorts, men and women in aprons or uniforms. Most were white, while several were black, Hispanic, or Asian. Normally, they would've staggered around without even noticing each other, but their hunger had united them in a way that would've been quite remarkable in life. The human species had finally overcome racism. Too bad we had to give up our intellect and turn into mindless cannibals to do so. The plausibility of the whole apocalypse/judgment thing occurred to me again as I turned away from them and grabbed the door handle.

The door was a big, heavy metal one. That was a huge bonus for me, as was the fact that it opened inward, though for the undead, these two facts slightly lessened their chance for lunch that day. Before the first zombie could figure out to push down on the thumb latch and pull the handle toward itself, the others would have pressed up against him and mashed him against the door in a writhing, moaning mass. Then the only way they were coming through the door would be when enough zombies in the back of the mob lost interest and wandered off, so that the pressure was taken off the front zombie and he could pull the door back. Given their monomania and their inability ever to get bored or distracted, that could take hours, if not days.

I squeezed the handle and yanked back on it. I couldn't afford to examine the alley behind the store before I went outside: so long as a bony hand didn't grab me immediately, I was going out that door.

No bony hand.

I stepped through the door and closed it.

With my left hand, I drew my knife—not the thin-bladed eye-poking one this time, but the big Crocodile Dundee-type one, the kind you could use to hack off a grasping hand, or bash-in the side of a zombie's head with the pommel. Within seconds, I heard the thumping of the dead assaulting the door from within, but as I had suspected, there was no sign that the door was opening.

At the end of the alley, several zombies were staggering toward me, and they let out a moan which would surely bring more. I had no choice but to go the other way, though this would probably take me farther into the city, which could be even worse. Again, there wasn't much choice. I ran that way till I reached the next cross street.

Zombies this time were everywhere, though there were definitely more to the left, closing in on where I had originally fired the shots. The farther I could get from that zombie magnet, the better my chances got, especially if I could do it without firing more shots.

I turned right and began running down that street. I dodged between the scattered undead, only once getting close enough to actually fight one off. It was an older woman, and it came around the front of a van that was up on the sidewalk as I ran between the vehicle and the building. The hair was matted to the left side of her head with blood from where her ear had been bitten off.

Her left arm reached out for me, clutching, even though much of the flesh of her forearm had been torn off, so much so that you could see the bones and tendons in her forearm moving back and forth. Her soulless moan sounded the alarm to any other zombies nearby.

"Die, bitch!" I growled as I brought my left hand up as hard as I could, driving the blade up under her chin until the tip of the blade shattered through the decayed top of her skull. I quickly drew the blade out and let her fall. For the first time that day, I felt exhilarated, and I almost wanted to spit on her body. I shivered at my reaction. Like the thousand yard stare, if you got the bloodlust, your chances of survival went down, because it made you careless and foolhardy. I wanted to get out of that town and to somewhere relatively safe before I descended further into that or some other species of madness.

I was making good and uneventful progress, not running too fast, conserving my strength, and not taking anymore shots that would draw more zombies. For almost a block, I was able to jump from the top of one wrecked car to another to avoid the grasping dead.

As I came over a rise, the street descended slightly to end in a cross street, beyond which was a park on the banks of a fairly large river. On the other side of the river looked to be a continuation of the park, and then lower buildings, not like the small downtown district I was in at the moment. The bridge across the river was one block to the left. All I had to do was run there, across the bridge, and I would be outside the city proper, on my way to the suburbs.

But as soon as I turned left, something moaned behind me. On the cross street that paralleled the river, at least a hundred zombies were heading my way.

I needed to get way ahead of them before nightfall, but that in itself was not a huge problem. Zombie top speed seemed to be about two miles per hour, so even a brisk walk—so long as you didn't get hung up with more obstacles—meant you could pull very far ahead of them in a short time, easily out of eyeshot. They weren't herd creatures by nature, which maybe says something about people—I don't know. They'd all follow the same goal, which was always the same: find someone to kill and eat. But they were never really a herd, much less a pack; they were just separate individuals who happened to be going in the same direction at the same time. And once the mob didn't see you, it would start to disperse. So as terrifying as a crowd of a hundred zombies looks, if you keep moving, it's not nearly as dangerous as a small crowd in an enclosed space, like I had just faced in the convenience store.

I kept running and made it to the bridge. It was a broad, low bridge, with four lanes plus a sidewalk on each side. At my end, a barricade had been built: two Humvees, parked perpendicularly across the roadway, supplemented with some cop cars, sand bags, concrete traffic barriers, and barbwire. It may well have held, for whatever good it had done, as the vehicles still effectively blocked the bridge. They did not appear to have been moved from their original spot, nor was there any sign of fire or explosion, common at such scenes.

The machine guns had been removed from the Humvees. It was probably just as well, in case I felt tempted to play Rambo and try mowing down the pursuing mob of zombies with a full auto weapon, a tactic that clearly hadn't worked for whoever had built the barricade, guys who probably had a lot more training than I did. For me, it would've been briefly satisfying on one level, but far more dangerous than simply retreating, as the noise would attract more and more of them from both sides of the river.

As usual when you came across a battle site, there weren't many bodies lying around, as most had gotten up and walked away, but there were a few scattered before the barricade, most in civilian garb, with a couple in military and police uniforms. There was no smell of decay, beyond the usual in a city of the dead, as the bodies had—unlike zombies—almost completely rotted away.

As was also usual at a battle site—I suppose from any war, but the war with the undead was the only one I knew—it was impossible to guess the details of what had gone on here: how many had fought, or died, or even whether the barricade had been intended to keep the undead on this side of the river, or to keep them from coming over from the other side.

Well, it all seemed pretty moot now. It was just a few vehicles and lifeless bodies, with weeds growing up through the cracks around them. It wasn't like there were going to be any people to make a monument here, like it was some kind of Gettysburg or Normandy. Just one of probably ten thousand places where the human race had just puttered out. In a few years, it'd be like finding the campsite and spearheads of some Neanderthals, the odd and poorly designed remnants of some species that didn't have what it takes to survive.

I looked back as I climbed over the barricade. Although, for the long haul, the dead seemed well-suited to survival, at the moment, they were falling behind me. The roadblock would probably slow them down enough that, by the time some of them made it over, I'd be way out of sight and they'd sit down on the bridge and forget all about me.

I ran across the bridge. The wrecked vehicles made it

impossible to see all the way to the other side, but there were no signs of zombies anywhere, and I almost started to relax. I looked down at the water, crystal clear and fast moving from the center of the channel to the far bank, shallower nearer the side I had left. I dodged past a few more vehicles and I was to the opposite side of the bridge. I could no longer see the barricade, but I was sure the dead had not surmounted that yet.

To my right was the park I had seen from the other side of the river, but to my left was a parking lot, beyond which was a high, brick wall, brightly painted. It ran from the river, along the parking lot, to where it connected to a large, irregularly-shaped brick building, maybe four stories tall. In the wall facing the parking lot, there was a large metal gate, while along the wall was spray painted "R U DYING 2 LIVE?" I wished I had time to ponder that, as it had been some time since I had someone other than myself to pose abstract questions, but there was an obvious impediment to such philosophizing—the crowd of zombies, probably almost two hundred, that was crowded in front of the wall, pressing against it.

They hadn't seen me yet. They were pretty intent on the wall, and they must've been for some time, as they weren't moaning or agitated, but just kind of milling around.

The street on this side was not as clogged with wrecked cars, so I couldn't dodge between them and hope to remain unseen. I would be running along an empty street, less than fifty yards from them. Still, if I just started running, I'd be in no worse situation than I was with the previous mob: I just had to keep running for long enough that I was out of their sight, then keep going till I was in a safer area. It was either that, or jump off the bridge into the river. Although the fall looked survivable, the chance of spraining an ankle, losing all my supplies and equipment, and coming up somewhere downstream that was just as bad made me think that it was not the better option.

I set off at a good sprint, trying to get as far down the street as I could before they started pursuit. Sure enough, after just a few yards, the moan started, and the chase was on. They turned, almost as a group, and begin staggering toward me. I kept running. But then another group emerged from a grove of trees and from behind a building in the park. It was just a dozen or so, nowhere near as big a mob as the zombies at the wall, but with just a few lurching steps, they had effectively cut off the street ahead.

I stopped. Now I either had to turn right, into the park, and hope the trees held no more surprises, or turn back and jump into the river. I didn't like either.

"You there!" an amplified voice called. The zombies stopped their march toward me, and I looked around. Over the top of the high brick wall, two platforms appeared on either side of the gate, the kinds of platforms on scissor-type lifts that people used to paint tall buildings or clean their windows. On each platform, two men stood, together with the .50 caliber machine guns from the Humvees. On the platform to my right was the guy with the bullhorn. I hadn't seen people in weeks, and these were, obviously, an especially welcome sight.

The zombies were temporarily frozen. It was one of the many disadvantages of almost completely lacking a working intellect—they couldn't handle multiple threats at all, or change from one target to another easily. They looked at their enemies above the wall, then back at me, swaying uncertainly. I, too, was frozen, as I wasn't sure at all what I was supposed to do. There were still about two hundred zombies, fanned out now in a more or less crescent-shaped wall of rotting, grasping flesh, between me and the people.

"Start moving toward the gate," the guy with the bullhorn said. "We're going to get you."

He sounded confident, and their set-up indicated a good deal of planning and equipment, like they had done this before, but I still wasn't too enthusiastic about moving toward a mob of mindless cannibals. I took a few slow steps, and again, the zombies moved toward me. But then we both heard the gate rattle as it slid to one side.

Again, the zombies were confused, and many at the back turned toward the gate. I took a few more steps, and then a crowd of about twenty people came rushing out from the gate. Like the guy on the cherry picker, they seemed pretty disciplined and organized, letting out a loud "Arrrrrr!" as they charged the zombies. They looked like the crazy, post-apocalyptic bikers and villagers in *The Road Warrior* movie, all decked out with various kinds of impromptu armor—football pads, paintball and fencing masks, pieces of tires cut up and bound to their arms and legs as armor, hubcaps and garbage can lids for shields. They crashed into the zombies, wielding bats, clubs, machetes, axes, shovels—any hand-to-hand weapon that could deal a fatal blow to the head.

The zombies were now completely confused, and they began to fall back before the assault. I was impressed and grateful for the people's bravery, but I didn't see how they stood a chance of clearing a path.

Up on the cherry pickers, the two people who were not on the machine guns were swinging things at the end of a rope, the way you would a sling, but the objects were bigger, so they were using both arms, like in a hammer throw. "Set!" the guy on the bullhorn commanded, and they let go their projectiles, which flew over the crowd and crashed down slightly in front of me, one to either side. When they hit the ground, I heard loud popping, and then splashing sounds. I wasn't sure, but I started to catch on, so I stopped and took a couple steps back.

The people who had thrown the objects were now wielding bows with flaming arrows, and from where I was standing, it looked like they were aimed right at me. I also got a whiff of something I hadn't smelled in years, that smell you always associated with summer evenings, when Dad went out and lit the Kingsford in the backyard. I kept backing up as the zombies again advanced on me.

"Fire!" came the command from the guy on the cherry picker, and the arrows shot into the zombie crowd right in front of me on either side. I ducked down, brought my right arm across my face, and hoped these people knew what they were doing.

Chapter Three

WHEN THE ARROWS hit and ignited the lighter fluid, the hair on the back of my hand singed and curled in the heat and blast of the expanding fire ball. Unlike the zombies, I needed to breathe, and I staggered back a step to catch my breath as the flames receded slightly after the initial flare up. The people in the cherry pickers pressed the attack, throwing another pair of fuel bombs, redoubling the flames and driving me another step back.

Just a few feet closer to the centers of the two conflagrations, the zombies were faring much worse than I. With their dried-up flesh and hair, most of them were burning briskly, and their moaning now turned to screams as they flailed about in whatever it was they experienced as pain. It smelled like a cross between a barbecue and the seventh circle of hell.

Though horribly burned, many of them were still capable of motion, with their limbs still moving, even though scorched bones could now be seen through their burned clothes and flesh. But even the more hardy ones were losing their struggle to carry on the fight, as their eyelids had shriveled up in the first blast of flame, and their eyeballs looked like singed marshmallows, with sizzling goo running down their dried, cracked cheeks. They would walk into each other, or collapse to their knees, their burning hands clutching their faces in a slow agony that looked appallingly like a final supplication to the God who had made them, punished them, and was now punishing them again.

Between the edges of the two puddles of burning fuel, there were only a few zombies who had completely escaped the flames. I started walking toward them, as this was the gap in the midst of the two burning mobs that led to the gates. The first zombie to get close to me I shot in the face, then kicked him in the stomach and sent him crashing into the burning zombies to my right. Unfortunately, another burning one grabbed my gun arm and lunged for it with its mouth. I twisted away as I drove my knife into its mouth. It flailed around, still burning, with the tip of my knife stuck in the back of its throat. I wrestled my right arm out of its grip and stuck the barrel in its left eye. I fired as I pulled my knife out, and the zombie fell back into the burning crowd.

This altercation had slowed me down, and two more were closing in, one from my left and the other right in front of me. The one on my left was horribly cadaverous, even by zombie standards. It had been a very old woman before its death, and from the look of its torso, it had been run over and crushed by some large vehicle since then. It couldn't move its arms, all its bones were so crushed, so its two limbs just hung at its sides, swaying randomly as it walked. Its dress was torn, revealing the shriveled, dried flesh underneath, crisscrossed with feathery lines of dried blood and caked with dirt. Its insatiable maw kept coming nevertheless, and would keep on doing so no matter what.

The one in front of me, on the other hand, was a fairly robust male, with just the typical neck wound and blood stain down his shirt. I leveled the Glock at him and fired, sending him falling back into another zombie behind him. At almost the same time, I slashed the old zombie's throat as hard as I could with the serrated back edge of my knife. The blow spun her around and dropped her, with her neck severed almost all the way to the spine. She landed on her face, but her head bounced up and twisted around, so she was looking completely backward, up at me, before the head flopped back down on its side.

Even then, she started to pull her knees up under herself and struggle to rise. She'd be able to get up, doubtless, but not before I got out of there.

There were just a few more zombies between me and the people who had come out from the gates. I kept moving, but the zombie that the robust male had fallen on was getting up, just as another was coming at me from the right. I kicked the rising one in the head as I shot the standing one in the face. I was just a few feet now from rescue, when something grabbed my left wrist.

I turned and raised the Glock, but saw that I was aiming too high. I was held by something less than four feet tall, what had been a little boy of six or seven. Its jugular was torn open on the left side, but there were no other marks on it. It was slowly bending its mouth toward my wrist, ignoring any danger I might pose in its obsession for human flesh, its only remaining goal or desire. I raised my left arm, lifting the child zombie off the ground even as it continued craning its neck, its bared teeth yearning for my arm.

Oddly enough, the color of this zombie's flesh was like that of milk, like all his blood had drained out when he died, but had not been replaced with the horrible putrefaction and discoloration that inevitably accompanied undeath, instead leaving him pristine and undefiled. Here was flesh without blood, but also flesh without decay. It was animal existence at its purest—deadly, unholy, and unstoppable.

I holstered the Glock and grabbed the horrible, beautiful thing by the throat as I wrenched my left arm free of its grip. I sheathed the knife and held the thing with both hands around its neck. It wouldn't have been so bad if I could've throttled it to end its eternally pitiable existence, letting it slip slowly into a merciful death, but zombie physiology wouldn't allow this. It didn't help that this thing in my hands was the same age as my youngest son last year. The only minuscule consolation was that he didn't look at me, but up at the sky, unblinking even though he stared right at the sun, his jaw still working in his hellish, animal hunger.

"Sorry" fell so far short of what was going on here and what I was feeling that I wasn't going to bother with it this time. "Damn you," I whispered instead, and I flung the little thing away from me and back into the flames. Damn who? The zombie? Me? God? The asshole who invented the disease that caused the dead to rise? What the hell, it looked like there was plenty of damnation to go around, so why not just damn us all together, Lord, in one big mass of suffering, with you as the King of it all. Unlike earlier that day, this time I really did feel nauseous.

Two of the people from the gate had reached me by this point. "Come on," one shouted, grabbing me by the shoulder, "let's get inside." I followed them dumbly through the gate as it rattled closed behind us.

Before me was a grassy area with several dozen people on it, as well as a few trees and some odd-shaped sculptures of metal and stone. It was enclosed by the brick wall behind us, which ran down to the river on the one side. To the right, meeting up with the wall, was the large building I had seen from outside. And about two hundred feet in front of me was another wall like the one behind us, again running from the building down to the river over there. The river was the fourth side of the enclosure.

The people who had brought me in were smiling and patting me, encouraged and pleased with their own work. But I was immediately met by a woman a little younger than I was, one who had not gone outside in the attack. Like everyone there, her garb was a hodgepodge of different outfits, but it definitely conveyed the sense of a scientist or doctor rather than a soldier—smiley-face hospital scrubs as pants, canvas loafers without socks, a stained man's dress shirt, and some kind of blue vest with pockets, sort of like the ones that greeters at Wal-Mart wear.

She looked me over. "Your arms, show me your arms," she said, not exactly gruffly, but definitely not friendly, either.

I rolled up my sleeves and showed my arms, turning them over, feeling very awkward and embarrassed. Nobody's hygiene had been what it should be since the dead rose, but you were still made aware of it at odd moments like this.

She had already moved on to my neck and torso, raising her eyebrows and looking down the front of my shirt, as well as tilting her head to see both sides of my neck. "No bites? You're sure you haven't been bitten?"

I knew she had to ask. After the initial outbreak, most people had been killed when someone in their group was bitten and they tried to take care of him, only to have him then rise as a zombie and attack the others. Almost all the hospitals were taken out in the first few hours because of that. And then once they realized how quickly it spread, people were faced with the awful burden of having to execute anyone who had been bitten. "No," I said, shaking my head, "nothing, I swear."

She kept looking me over, though she still didn't feel bold enough to touch me in order to turn me around or lift my clothing. "No fever, chills, burning thirst, loss of appetite, vomiting?"

I kept shaking my head. "No, really."

"Open your mouth." I did. She winced. "Not the prettiest sight, but whose mouth is these days with no running water or toothpaste?"

She tried a different tactic. "Don't be afraid to tell us if you're sick, we won't send you back outside. We're not barbarians. We'll treat you humanely. We've quarantined people before. Some even pulled through."

"No they didn't," a voice behind me said. The guy who had been giving the orders on the bullhorn was walking up to us. He was big, not body-builder big, but a little taller than me, and he had obviously been in shape before months of tight rations and fighting off those things had whittled him down a bit. Now he just looked sort of gaunt and tenacious. He was about my age, late thirties, and dressed in the remnants of a military uniform, though I don't think the various parts matched or were from the same branch of the service.

Again, I didn't know much about the military or wars before the one we were in right then, and in this one we couldn't stand much on conventions. It was amazing and welcomed just to meet people who had a pulse. If they had themselves a little compound with a wall and some weapons and supplies, they could dress like the archbishop of Canterbury or flaming drag queens—or, what the hell, even both—it made absolutely no difference. Which meant, of course, that it never really did.

Oddly, the presence of a never-sleeping army of the undead just outside the gates really didn't change the dynamics of petty squabbles and insults and power plays, so the woman, whose pride was somehow hurt by the remark, shot back, "Yes, that one guy did!"

Military guy smiled. "Okay, Jones did, because he was just barely nicked on the hand and you chopped his damn arm off at the shoulder about two minutes after he'd been bitten. It was so tiny he might've pulled through with his arm if you hadn't. Don't sugarcoat it for this guy."

The woman flushed. "I did the best I could! I always do the best I can, you macho asshole! I was a damn dental hygienist before . . . before . . . Oh, why do you have to be so *mean*?!" Her voice was starting to crack and she turned and stomped off.

There was an awkward silence. I was glad that their military precision was better honed than their interpersonal skills, or I probably would've been incinerated, or eaten, or both. "I'll go talk to her later," he said, a little surprising and almost comical in his sheepish contrition. "We call her Doc, even though she's . . . well, you heard that she's not completely, all the way, exactly . . . a doctor. But we try to be nice to her and show her some respect, 'cause she's helped a lot of people. Damn it, I shouldn't have said anything." Another awkward silence. "You'll have to excuse us, but it's just hard with new people. It's so embarrassing, admitting how little we have here and how many things we can't do, and how scared we all are. But we have to be careful."

"No, no, I understand. What you did was amazing, and I'm grateful you got me in time."

He picked himself up a little, forgetting his faux pas and reasserting some authority. "But she's right—if you're bitten or hurt or sick, we'll do the best we can for you, even if we have to quarantine you." He took a step toward me. "But if you lie about it and we find out, it'll be different."

I wasn't trying to be a bad ass, but I sensed this guy was again jockeying for position, and I still understood enough about people to know that I had to have some credibility and respect in this new group, so I met his gaze and didn't back down. "I said I understood."

We'd gotten our male posturing out of the way early, and to everyone's satisfaction, which seemed to suit him fine. He stuck out his hand. "Sorry. I'm Jack Lawson."

We shook hands. "Jonah Caine," I said.

We walked over to a table near the gate where a young man sat with a clipboard. On one side of him, one of those big Rubbermaid storage sheds shelved dozens of weapons, and on the other side there was a big plastic garbage can. The people who had attacked the zombies at the gates were handing in their weapons to the man at the table, and he was marking them down and putting them in the locker. They tossed their armor and shields and larger items into the garbage can.

Jack put his own pistol, an old Colt .45, on the table. He turned to me. "Rules. You'll have to hand over your weapons. We'll keep them and give them back if you ever want to leave."

This was a little more than just looking me over for bites, more than them protecting themselves; this was them asking for a lot of my trust so they could enforce some crazy rules they'd thought of for their group. And it was taking away the only things that had kept me alive for weeks. "I'm not handing over my weapons. What if they break in? I don't know how safe this place is."

"It's plenty safe, trust me. We can't always go outside whenever we want, but they can't get in. And we're rigged up pretty good if they do. There are weapons lockers all over the compound, and they're all guarded, but you'll never be far from a gun or a club if you need to defend yourself. You saw how many of us could get armed and go get you, as soon as our lookouts spotted you. It's just part of our community that when we're in here, we don't want to have weapons to remind us of how we have to live, or to ever tempt us to use them on each other. We don't have much here, but we don't have to live like people used to." He paused, and we were once again back to posturing, unfortunately. "It's not a request."

"I know." I put the Glock, the magnum, and four knives on the table.

"Anything else in the bag?"

"Just clothes and food and stuff, no weapons."

"Okay." He made a gesture, and a boy of about thirteen came running up. "Is it all right if he takes the bag inside?" he asked me. He looked at the boy and made his tone stern. "He knows not to open it."

"Sure," I agreed. The boy took my backpack and ran off toward the building.

Jack eased up a little and visibly relaxed. "Well, welcome to our little place. Let's take a walk around."

We headed toward the river. "Jonah . . . Jonah . . . Wasn't he in the Bible? Didn't he—no, Noah was the guy in the ark, with the animals. What did Jonah do?"

"Jonah was swallowed by a whale."

"I thought that was Pinocchio."

"Him too."

"Oh, yeah, right." He laughed a little. So did I, for the first time in weeks.

"What was this place?" I asked, looking around.

Jack stopped and turned, pointing back at the big building. Near the top was a large sign that read, "MUSEUM OF SCIENCE AND HISTORY." Jack laughed again. "It was kind of a miscellaneous museum for the whole area, since they didn't have too much of either science or history that was unique to here." He gestured to the sculptures we were walking by. "I'm not sure how these qualify as either science or history, but they eventually added the sculpture garden, too. No big discoveries or battlefields or artists around here, but they had some nice displays. Kids liked it. We all used to come here when we were kids, and some of the older people in our group used to bring their kids here. And being by the river was always nice. They'd have concerts in the summer, and you'd come down to see the fireworks over the river on the Fourth of July. Now it's all we have. I guess it's not where any of us would've picked to be when the world ended, but it's held up pretty good."

We had reached a low fence and hedge that bordered the river. I looked over and saw that we were at the top of a concrete wall that dropped about six feet down to the water. It was an unusually good setup for defense against attackers who didn't have weapons or vehicles or machines. It almost seemed fated, or even providential. But I couldn't quite make myself believe it, even though I partly wanted to.

Over the hedge and fence, there was a string, with various bells and wind chimes every couple feet. Jack held one to show me. "Just in case. We keep a close eye on this point, since it's not perfectly secure. Sometimes, one of them will manage to climb around the edge of the wall. Usually they just fall in the water and the current takes them downstream, but a couple have gotten a foot up on the wall here and have grabbed on to the hedge before somebody whacked them and killed them."

"How'd you all get set up here?" I asked. "We heard on the radio and TV to go to military outposts, forts, those kinds of things."

Jack looked down at the water, then across the river at the city. "Yeah, for the first few days, that made sense. If there are corpses walking around and the only way to stop them is to shoot them in the head, then it made sense to go somewhere where there are lots of guys with guns."

He sighed. "But as the tide turned, those became death traps. All those people in one place, shooting guns and making noise, and driving and flying vehicles in and out: the dead converged on them and overwhelmed them. Whoever could get out and make a stand somewhere else, did. No, an army camp in the states hasn't been set up for a siege since the days of cowboys and Indians.

"Nowadays, they just have barbed wire fences and gates with some barricades you have to drive around. Hell, they were set up for stopping suicide truck bombers, not armies of walking corpses. What the hell does a zombie care about a waist high concrete barrier or spikes that shred your tires? He doesn't know what tires are anymore."

He fell silent for a second, but then he laughed again and

gestured at the walls, and I definitely got the feeling that he thought of them as *his* walls. "No, if you needed a place that was made for keeping people out, and you were lucky and it hadn't already been blown open or burned down, the place to look was where they used to charge *admission*! And preferably a place where not too many people would think to hole up. At least there you would have a shot. We got lucky."

He looked at me quizzically for a moment. "Or God was looking out for us? You believe in God, Jonah?"

I looked down at the rushing water. I didn't know the answer to his question. If I were being practical, I might have thought just to tell him what he wanted to hear, whether it was true or not, but I wasn't sure yet from his comments what he thought the right answer to his question was. "I don't know. I'm sorry."

He took it in stride. I was beginning to get the impression that he took a lot in stride, and I liked that. "No need to be sorry. I'd think you were crazy or retarded if you could answer that with two thumbs up or two thumbs down at this point." He looked so thoughtful, gazing across the river at the city of the dead. "No, I think this has definitely taken all the certainty out of it, if you ever had any. You think of all the good people, the honest and kind people, who've died since this began, and you just can't help thinking the Big Guy is on vacation and he left the other guy in charge. What do they call that?"

I knew the Bible a little, but I wasn't up on all the end of the world stuff. "The Apocalypse?"

"No, no, I had an aunt who was into all that junk. . . . It was a special part of the apocalypse. . . . Oh, yeah, the 'Tribulation' she called it, when the Beast would rule the world for seven years. Anyway, you see this and you think either there isn't a God, or if there is, then He must be taking a big, divine siesta, and we're catching hell—literally—until he wakes up.

"But then you look at something like this," again, the gesture to his walls, his domain, and he clearly wasn't just proud of it, he was grateful for it, and would even pray for it, if he could, "and you know we'd all be dead if it weren't for a million little coincidences and lucky breaks, and you can't help thinking maybe, just maybe we'll make it, and we were supposed to make it, and it'll all work out."

Jack was getting his own thousand yard stare, I could see. In his position, he probably had to give a lot of pep talks and bolster people's courage in tough times, so he hadn't had a chance to speak his real, more ambiguous and pained mind in days.

"Well, Jonah, to go back to your question: everything here kind of came together haphazardly, little by little. For the first couple days, there were just a few museum employees holed up here. They grabbed all the food from the cafeteria that they could, and they barricaded themselves on the top floor. As they looked out the windows, though, they got a little braver. They saw that nobody—living or dead—was paying any attention to them, and so long as they stayed away from the windows and doors in the main lobby that face the outside street—don't worry, we walled those up later—they could move all over the museum and the grounds.

"They got brave enough to open the gates—there's another gate to the employee's parking garage in the back—to let in survivors sometimes. Fortunately, they only did that after they'd heard on the radio and TV about the bites, so they knew to be careful. They were brave people. They even went up to the roof."

He pointed to a little glass enclosure on top of the building. "See that? The local TV station had a camera up there. It'd show you a view of downtown all the time on their website, and they'd show the view from it at the end of the 11 o'clock news. Before the electricity went off, the people got brave enough—or lonely enough—to stand in front of it and try to get out a message that there were people here and it was fairly safe and they'd try to let you in. Fortunately, not too many people saw it, or tried to get here, or it probably would've been mobbed by the living, and then by the dead, and there'd be nothing here now.

"A few days into it, we showed up—the military. We also didn't think anything of one more shut-up building, and we drove right by here without a thought. We rounded up some police and firemen who were still listening to their radios, and we built the barricade you probably saw on the bridge. We were sent to try and keep the dead in the city.

"At first, it was easy. Shoot one every couple minutes, wait, shoot another. But little by little, you were shooting them constantly, and they were still coming. It was obvious we couldn't stay there. We were the only ones still trying to hold on to one of the bridges, so they could just get around us on another bridge and come at us from behind. I know, I know, they couldn't figure that out as a conscious strategy, but the point is, our position was exposed, and it wasn't even keeping the dead in the city, since they had other ways out.

"We knew we had to get out of there, but at that point, we'd stopped hearing anything from our base. The crowds of dead were getting bigger, and we had no idea where to fall back to. It was then that somebody saw people on the shore here, pretty much right where we're standing now. You know, from a distance, you can't tell if it's a real person or one of them, but through binoculars you could, and we could see they were real people, alive and waving. We were lucky: we were able to pull back and only lost a few men. We even retrieved the .50 calibers from the Humvees and a lot of ammo. God knows, we've needed it since.

"We waited with the people who were already here, listening to the radio and watching the TV. But in a few days, there was nothing. You didn't hear shots in the distance or explosions anymore, either. It was just still, just the sound of the river, with the reeking of the dead rolling across you when the wind shifted. And at that point, supplies became an issue.

"We were a lot luckier than some people, because we had the river for water. But all we had to eat was what had been raided from the museum snack bar and whatever people had brought with them when they'd been let in. So we launched raids for supplies.

"We got better organized as time went on. Like I said, we walled up the lobby completely, so we had no worries there. There was construction going on at the museum when the outbreak began, so there were some construction supplies to do the work, as well as the cherry pickers you saw, and we could see how to use those to defend the gates when we needed to open them. We got especially good at distracting the stiffs—setting up a ruckus out by the employee parking lot till they all congregated there, then launching a raid out the main entrance, or vice versa. We can go through the sewers to a couple spots on this side of the river.

"Oh, and to the other side of the river?" He got a mischievous grin. "See that?" He pointed overhead to a wire that ran from the roof of the museum to the city on the other side.

"That was my idea: a zip line. I swam across during the night and waited till dawn, then climbed out and tied the thing down, so we'd always have a way to get to the other side quickly. It's another way we set up distractions for the stiffs. Cool?"

"Very cool, Jack." I was truly impressed with everything, and also didn't want to let him down, as he was obviously getting wound up.

"For a while, we kept picking up survivors. At first, there were quite a few. We'd spot smoke somewhere and go check it out and bring a few people back. That's how we got Popcorn and Tanya."

"Popcorn?"

"Long story. Somebody will explain it to you when you meet him. Sometimes, someone would get close, and we'd let them in, like we did you. That's how we got Milton. You'll meet him later. He's kind of important."

"Important? Important how? Like a leader?"

"No, not exactly. It's another long story. I'm sorry, it seems like everything here is a long story, but that's just how everything's come together in a little less than a year, and it's hard to explain in a few minutes. So anyway, we've been scrounging for supplies, but this year might be better. We've caught some fish from the river, and now we're going to try growing some vegetables here, so we might eventually not be so reliant on Spam and Twinkies."

"I was getting tired of them, too."

"I know, a hazard of the apocalypse."

"Who put the sign up outside?"

He laughed again. "Our little motto, or half of it? Milton thought of it, to let people know there's someone still in here, and to say we're dying to really live, not just living to die."

"I hope that's not his most profound idea."

Jack laughed harder. "No, not at all. He's got some odd ones, I'll admit, but they all kind of work out and make sense. I don't know how to explain him, either, but you'll see. I'm kind of the joint chiefs of staff or the secretary of state, and he's more like the pope or the dalai lama."

I thought about that for a second. "Who's the president in that scenario?"

"That's one we haven't had so much use for in our new setup."

This time we both laughed, and more heartily.

Chapter Four

WE WALKED BACK toward the museum. The side of the building that faced the river and sculpture garden was all windows, with glass doors near the front wall. Jack led me through these into the lobby, a large circular room that extended the height of the building, with a huge Calder-inspired mobile hanging in the midst of it.

I could see the construction Jack had spoken of—roughly made brickwork had been erected on the inside, shutting off the large windows and doors that fronted on the street outside. At irregular intervals, some bricks had been left out at eye level, to function as peepholes, I assumed, and possibly gun-slits, if it came to that. Walling it in had made the room dark and cavernous, though the sun was now shining in from the western side of the building, over the dead city and across the river and sculpture garden. As Jack had promised, there was another weapons locker here, with a young man seated next to it.

From the lobby, a spiral staircase ascended to the second, third, and fourth floors, and a large archway led into a huge room on the first floor. A sign above the archway read, "MAIN EXHIBIT HALL." Jack and I went up the staircase, all the way to

the fourth floor. After the third, the sign above the stairs read, "EMPLOYEE OFFICES."

"We kept their original idea of barricading ourselves in on the top floor," Jack said. You could tell that he loved arranging and organizing things, and then describing the arrangements and all the thought that had gone into them. "If the stiffs ever got this far, I don't suppose it would make much difference, but I think it helps if people think there's a plan. Without electricity, the staircase is the only way up, except for the fire stairs at the end of the hall. Those are sealed up on the lower floors, so you can only get to them from up here, and they lead up to the roof, so we could fall back to there if we ever had to."

"All you need is a helicopter."

Jack looked around and gestured toward the ceiling. "I don't think the roof would take a big one, one big enough for everyone, but maybe a small one. Hey—are you making fun of me?"

I smiled. "Only a little. I actually think a helicopter would be good, as a last resort, and possibly for getting supplies, too."

"Well, I'll put that on my to-do list." He went back to his tour. "This is where most everybody sleeps, unless they're on duty. We run three shifts, same as people used to on bases or factories or wherever. If someone petitions me and Milton, sometimes we let people bunk on the lower floors. Real estate here isn't at too much of a premium. People still need some privacy, especially if we're going to start having babies."

I knew how unlikely but inevitable that seemed. "Has that happened yet?"

He smiled, part lascivious, part humorous, part just happy. "Yes, just a few, and more on the way." But the smile faded. "But not nearly as many as we've planted in the ground out by the sculptures, or burned up out back in the parking lot. We bury our dead, even if they've turned, but we don't bury any zombies we kill attacking the place. I guess it's not fair, but it doesn't seem right, treating them like people, when you didn't know them when they were people."

"I suppose not." I began to realize how many of the finer points of living and undeath I had missed, surviving on my own.

There were people milling about near the other end of the hall. They stayed back, though some looked our way. Jack opened the door to a very small office, in which the desk and furnishings had all been pushed to one corner. The window was open and what looked like a very old Native American blanket lay on the floor, with my backpack next to it. "This is kind of our guest room, for new people till they're more used to us and we're used to them. We took the blanket from a display, obviously. We've ended up using a lot of the displays for one thing or another. I guess we should be trying to preserve them better."

"I'm sure you're doing fine." I picked up my backpack and unzipped it. "I assume you have some rule about sharing food?"

"Yes, that was one of the first, even before the weapons rule. I guess someday our Bill of Rights will be in one of the displays."

I held the bag open, showing a couple dozen snack cakes on top. "Well, I don't know how you're going to carry these to wherever you'd put them."

He laughed. Looking around, he reached over to the desk and grabbed one of those baskets that people use to hold papers and mail. I loaded it up, eventually uncovering the bottle of bourbon underneath.

"Whoa," Jack whispered when he saw it, looking around, partially closing the door, and setting down his basket of snack cakes. "Now, now, let's not get too carried away with all this stuff about everyone sharing everything. You said *food*, not *booze*. Giving everyone a thimbleful, versus giving two or three people a chance to forget their problems for one evening—well, I think that's an easy matter of weighing the greater good for the greatest number, don't you?"

"I leave that up to your leadership, Jack. I don't want to cause trouble. I'll pour it out on the ground if you want."

He looked at me and raised an eyebrow. "Now I know you didn't just say that. I'd write a new law myself telling what happens to people who are crazy enough to waste booze." He pulled the bottle out of the bag. When he saw the brand, he wrinkled his nose. "I hope you didn't risk your life for *this*?"

I laughed. "No, no, it was lying right out in the open."

"I can see why." Then he shrugged. "Well, we've made due with a lot worse inconveniences than bad booze." He slipped it into an inside pocket of his camouflage jacket. "Let's just not mention this to anyone and see if we can maybe enjoy it a little later on with some young ladies I know."

"I wouldn't want to intrude, Jack. You already said how important privacy is in those situations."

He laughed harder than he had all afternoon. "Oh, God, don't worry about that. I'm going to go talk to Doc, just to make sure she'll even talk to me anymore, and Tanya's made it clear that the only men she likes less than soldiers are cops. If anybody's going to be asking the other guy to make himself scarce so he can get lucky, it'll be you."

"Then why are you inviting them?" I asked, laughing along with him.

He turned suddenly serious, and since we were alone, I was pretty sure it wasn't going to be bluster or posturing. "Because I mostly talk to the people here my age, the ones who've seen things and lost things and been hurt and who probably aren't ever going to come through to the other side of this and become the new Adam or Eve. Those two gals are like that. And I don't mean to put you down, but I'm thinking that describes you pretty closely, too."

"I understand, Jack. It's not a put down; it's just the way it is."

"Good," he said, brightening up again. "So I guess all I'm saying is, I wouldn't mind talking to you and them and sharing your booze, and I'm not going to fight you for any of the gals here, though you'll have to excuse me if I still try to talk a big game—a man's got to have some pride left. If the youngsters want to go off and repopulate the earth, I'm perfectly happy to be guarding the gate from those things while they do it." He leaned a little closer. "All the more reason not to begrudge me a few drops of bad booze."

He picked up his office basket of snack cakes and started to leave. "Meet me back in the lobby a little after sundown."

"Thanks, Jack."

"See you in a bit."

After Jack left, I circulated some on the fourth floor. There were many larger offices with several people living in each, and two really big rooms in which they had rearranged the cubicle partitions to make them into living space. Everyone was friendly, though they clearly had some boundaries and some set rituals and restraints about getting to know newcomers. Given Jack's description of the growth of their community, I seemed to be the first new addition for some time, so that probably made it more difficult. On the other hand, it also made me quite the object of curiosity, so everyone was eager, if not to get to know me, then at least to see me and say hello.

Before it got too awkward talking to people in the living quarters, I made my way back to the sculpture garden and down to the river's edge. The sun was lowering in the sky, just sinking beneath the tops of the buildings across the river. City skylines were perhaps one of the most remarkable and disorienting sights in the world of the dead. During the daylight hours, the line of tall buildings was probably not that different from how it had appeared in the city of the living, but at night, it became one big, black, silent outline of rectangular shapes against the stars, sort of the way mountains looked at night, except mountains were never so angular, and one didn't expect them to twinkle cheerfully with thousands of lights. Such weird, artificial shapes as the outlines of big buildings demanded the softening, gladdening glow of artificial light to make them bearable. Without it, they became oppressive, monstrous, nightmarish. And in the gloom of twilight, as now, the nightmare was taking hold of the city.

The river, on the other hand, had retained its beauty, or the darkness had even enhanced it. In the city of the living, the river would have been a cold, dark void under the banks and the bridge. But now, it was the city that was dark and threatening, while the river's constant murmuring was a comforting, lulling blanket, taking my mind off of the dead, who were blessedly silent now after our battle, however many of them were still left out there.

As I gazed at the water, I thought of how it would reflect

the stars and the moon later this evening, the only visible sign that perhaps the hellish, cannibal earth would ever again reflect the quiet peace of heaven. Certainly none of the edifices of man on the other side of the river had ever done that: now they were just part of a giant, broken corpse, madly swarming with thousands of little, insane corpses. I shook off that thought and focused back on the river. After a moment I smiled, having forgotten how much water always calmed me.

It was getting dark. I turned back to the museum, seeing a few lights. I walked back to the lobby and found Jack, who led me into the main exhibit hall. With its ceiling four stories high, the side of the hall that faced the river was all windows. The room was lit with many candles and a few large torches, and there were many round tables laid out with folding chairs.

In the gloom above, I could just make out a biplane and the skeleton of a mosasaur, hanging from the ceiling. To see an ancient fighter plane and the skeleton of a prehistoric reptile by flickering torchlight made the place feel like a cross between Valhalla and a ride at Epcot—not creepy so much as surreal, almost funny. The reality, doubtless, was less grandiose and less comical.

"Big fundraiser tonight, Jack?"

"What? Oh, the tables. Yeah, darndest thing, isn't it? We found all these tables in a big storage area. Now we take our common meals here."

I laughed a little. "I volunteered at a museum years ago, and they all have their most impressive, breathtaking hall set up to hold fundraising banquets for rich donors."

"Yeah, the employees here told us, but it's still funny. They'll never have another fundraiser or rich person in here, and they've just got to trust us to be careful when we're sleeping on the ancient Indian blankets and cooking in some antique copper pot."

"I forgot to ask: is this where I'll meet Milton?"

"No, I was hoping you might, but he's sick again. I talked to him and he said tomorrow definitely."

"Sick?"

"It's another of those things that's really hard to explain around here. He's not going to turn, if that's what you mean, Jonah. I keep telling you—a million little accidents that keep us alive, and Milton's like the biggest one of them all. But you just wait till tomorrow for him."

Jack led me to a serving line where we got the usual post-apocalyptic fare: Spam, canned vegetables, and canned fruit. The one surprise was some flat, slightly burnt biscuits. I hadn't had anything even pretending to be bread in months, and I would gladly have taken more than the two I was given. It was funny, but before all this, you wouldn't have thought bread could ever be an interesting food, but as with the river, its simple attractiveness had been enhanced.

After the serving line, Jack led me to a table where I recognized Doc, though she had shed the blue vest and had changed into a sweatshirt from the museum's gift shop. I learned her real name, Sarah, and it fit her perfectly: ordinary, capable, solid. She was a lanky woman, and the shirt looked slightly too small for her because she had rolled up the sleeves. So that they wouldn't come to just below her elbows, I suspected. Her hair wasn't pulled back into a ponytail as before, and you could see she might have been pretty before all this. She was still self-conscious, but Jack clearly had made amends with her, and she was much more at ease in this setting.

With her was an African-American woman who remained,

even in her disheveled state, quite striking. This was the Tanya that Jack had mentioned. She was only slightly shorter than I was, about my age, with her hair closely shorn, and she had the toned but not bulky body of a swimmer or gymnast. She was slightly butch, to be honest, and reminded me of my gym teacher in middle school.

She seemed somehow to be less haggard than the rest of us, without the clear weight loss, sunken cheeks, and the dulled gaze. Tanya's eyes were deep and brown and infinitely soothing, but full of life. To be honest, she reminded me of the Homeric tag-line "ox-eyed Hera," like she was meant to look down on mere mortals. More than anyone I'd seen for months, more than I had thought possible anymore, she exuded vitality.

But when Jack introduced me, there was something pained and forced in her smile, and I could tell immediately she never laughed. Here was the pain and loss of which Jack had spoken, the misery that put us all in the same category and allowed us to communicate and sympathize. I could see the truth of Milton's little riddle or motto: about a year ago, we all had died, and now we were just living to die a final time.

Morbid thoughts notwithstanding, we were all in the mood to have as good a time as we could at our table. I don't think it would be possible to *savor* such fare as we had, but we did linger on it, not so much to enhance any flavor, but just because the prevailing wisdom held that it made you feel fuller for longer if you took your time, while wolfing it down was supposed to make you hungry again sooner. As with all such folk wisdom, though, there were proponents of both sides.

Jack was all business at dinner, but in a jovial way. "I was especially glad with how fast we got out to you," he said. "We practice it a lot, but I was afraid, since we hadn't done it in so long, that you'd be running around out there for a lot longer before we got enough people to the gate. And the fire—they did really good this time. We have to practice that with watered-down paint, but we don't do it so much, 'cause it gets the neighbors all riled up, obviously. But they really got the two kill zones nicely spaced—just enough room in between for you to get in."

Slightly less morose and a little more playful than I'd seen her, Sarah said, "Enough, Jack, it's not a post-game show." .

"I know, I know. But, hey—Jonah here brought us something special, and I was wondering if you ladies would join us over in Frontierland to see it?"

"It better not be anything disgusting," Tanya said, "or I'll put a hurt on you." She was also a little more playful. "And you too, new guy," she added, glaring at me, "even if G. I. Joe here put you up to it."

"Nothing of the kind," I reassured them.

"Meet us there in five," Jack said, and he and I left to take our dishes back.

On our way to the rendezvous, Jack turned on a flashlight and led me through some much smaller exhibit halls. "We try to conserve batteries as much as possible," he whispered as we walked past cases of Native American artifacts, "but walking with a candle is just too damned hard."

After two more rooms of artifacts, we entered the recreated interior of a frontier cabin. Jack lit a couple candles and placed the bottle on the roughhewn table, then arranged four mismatched mugs of pewter, glass, and porcelain around it. We sat down, and a couple minutes later, Sarah and Tanya entered from the cabin's other entrance.

Both women gave the requisite "Oooh," at the sight of booze, like teens at a party about to do something wrong and forbidden and dangerous. As I watched them, I finally figured out what I had been going over in my mind at dinner—how the two of them complemented each other. Sarah was by far the more nervous of the two—even now, she was glancing about, just like a kid worried about being caught at his illicit activity—while Tanya was utterly unflappable. If anybody complained to her about her drinking, she'd break the bottle over his head.

Sarah, on the other hand, could be saddened more easily, but she could also be more easily cheered, while inside Tanya there was clearly such a well of pain and anger that it was almost uncomfortable to be around her, as bold and vivifying as she was.

But as nervous or sad as they were, there was something infinitely comforting—in an emotional, if not sexual, way—about having them around, as Jack had tried to describe before. Their attractiveness, too, had been enhanced by our horrible situation.

Jack played host, pouring the bourbon. "To new friends." We all toasted and took our first drink in ages.

Somewhat predictably, the women's drinking was opposite as well: Sarah barely sipped, Tanya slammed the booze down. Till it kicked in, we didn't talk much. I knew when Jack suggested the get-together that that was part of the value of the booze—to get people to talk.

About halfway into the bottle, Sarah spoke up. "So, Jonah, what's your story? How'd you get here? People say you came

from a secret underground bunker, or that you fought your way out of an overrun military base, or God knows what else."

"I was on a ship when it started," I said. The bourbon had done the trick, as I would otherwise have shrugged it off with something vague.

"You were like in the Navy or something?" Sarah asked. "What's that group? The SEALS? That's what someone was guessing."

Jack guffawed. "No, he was most definitely *not* a SEAL. No offense, Jonah."

"I know. . . . No, nothing military. I'm . . . well, I *was* a college English professor, just working at a community college, and I'd work on cargo ships during the summer for extra money."

"Family?" Tanya asked, between gulps.

"Yes, a wife and two kids. The ships paid better than teaching summer school, so I was doing it until I could get a better position. The disease must've broken out right after we got on board. Just the day after we left L.A., the television and radio were talking about it. We just thought it was local and we'd go ahead to Honolulu and everything would be normal. But then it was obviously not. The captain just stopped the ship, and we watched and listened to the reports. Until they stopped. We'd still get short wave stuff, but we didn't know what was going on, all just garbled cries for help.

"We sailed back to within sight of the docks. There were fires everywhere, and we got our first look at . . . them. You'd think they were people at first, of course, but then we'd see them through the binoculars, and we'd understand what the TV had been talking about. We sailed up the coast, still hoping the reports were wrong and it was just in the city, but it was everywhere—fires, and those things staring at us from the shore. You didn't see anything human on the shore, but a few survivors in boats pulled up alongside us. We'd heard about the bites, so we didn't let any infected on board, fortunately.

"Little by little, we had a flotilla or colony floating around out there offshore. But after a couple weeks, no more showed up, like Jack said happened with you guys here. We'd share supplies, fish for food, and some of the guys rigged up a distillery to desalinate the water. I guess it was as safe as we could hope for, but some of us with families weren't satisfied. We had to know if they were still alive, if they made it."

"I know," Jack sighed. "It's a pull, a pull too strong for some people, stronger than the will to survive. We had people leave to look for family. None of them ever came back. I hope they found them and are off on an island somewhere."

"Me too, but we all know the chances of that." I took a gulp. "Those of us who wanted to leave took some supplies, guns, and one of the smaller boats. We found a place to land where we didn't see any of them, and we went our separate ways to look. I don't know what happened to any of the others, but I stayed alive and kept looking. I found my town, found my house. Nothing there. No bodies, no blood, the car was gone, but what does that prove? Just that they didn't die in the house. After that, I didn't know what to do, so I just wandered. And that's pretty much how I ended up on your doorstep. Sorry, it's nothing too dramatic, I guess."

We were silent for a while. "I was at work," Sarah said very quietly. "Me, and the doctor, and the receptionist."

"I thought you said you were a dental hygienist?" I asked.

"The dentists usually prefer to be called 'doctor.' It was a crowded little strip mall, and it all went to hell in a couple hours, with people outside being attacked in the parking lot, cars crashing, explosions, sirens, gunshots. We just locked the doors and drew the blinds and watched the TV. I'm sorry, it seems so cowardly now, like I should've tried to help or do something."

Jack and Tanya both knew to put their hands on her shoulders. "It's okay, baby," Tanya whispered. "You did plenty here. Everyone knows. You just hold on to that."

Sarah resumed. "But when the TV started saying that we were supposed to get to a rescue station, they wanted to make a run for it. His car was parked close, and it really looked like maybe we could make it. This was just the first day, so we didn't know about . . . we didn't know that they . . . you know . . ."

"That they rip your guts out and eat them while you're still watching," Jack muttered, looking into his cup. Tanya glared at him.

"Yes, I think they wouldn't have tried it if they knew that. The people we had seen attacked in the parking lot, it just looked like they were fighting with them, and then they'd fall behind a car or something. We didn't know. And the TV hadn't said anything about that. They just said to go to a rescue station. So they wanted to try it. I just couldn't. I told them that I couldn't, that I'd just freeze and scream. So they said okay, they'd go and send back help later.

"They tried it, and I just closed and locked the door behind them. There were so many of those things in the parking lot that we hadn't seen, and they got them. And I saw it all. It was quick, at least. I don't know what I would've done if it hadn't been quick."

She stopped and put her head on Tanya's shoulder. Then she picked back up. As I had thought, she was quick to break down, but more resilient in coming back. She took a sip of the bourbon. "I'm okay, thanks. I was in the office for a while. It seemed like forever. I didn't make a sound, after I saw what had happened to them. I barely moved or breathed.

"When I saw there were none of them right outside, I wrote 'HELP' on the window with lipstick. I filled a bunch of containers with water before the water stopped running, but I didn't have food. I tore the place apart and just found the usual stuff that you throw in a drawer and forget about—little bags of saltines or oyster crackers, ketchup and sugar and soy sauce packets, the after dinner mints you get from restaurants. I ate the damn fern we had growing on the counter. I was pretty weak when the people from here picked me up."

The silence was a little longer this time, and then, inevitably, Tanya spoke. "I was at home. In the kitchen. No TV on. It was summer. I didn't let the kids hardly watch TV. But then I heard them scream. First one, then the other. They came running in, all bloody. They were babbling something crazy about the neighbor bit them and they ran away from him. They both had what looked like teeth marks on their arms. I was looking at them when the neighbor came through the door, all weird and crazy-looking and covered with blood.

"I pushed my babies behind me and told them to go upstairs and lock themselves in the bathroom. He was coming toward us, mouth open, all drooling and shit. He was bit too, on the neck, I could see, but I didn't care about him. I grabbed the frying pan and told him to just stop, I was going to call the police. But he was between me and the phone anyway, and I already thought that this was way past what the police could do anything about.

"He came at me, and I kicked him in the nuts, but he didn't even flinch. Nothing. Like I'd kicked the damned wall next to him and not him. He kept coming at me, and I gave him the frying pan across the head. Hard. And two more times. The first two times I heard a crunch, and the last time it sounded wet and squishy. He went down. The blood started seeping out from under him, all thick and dark. The kitchen looked like a damned horror movie, with all the blood from my kids and him. I dragged him outside quick and locked all the doors.

"I thought to get my babies to a hospital, but then I looked outside and there were more of those things in the street. Just like Sarah said—cars crashing, houses on fire, shooting, all hell breaking loose. I turned on the TV and started to see what was going on. Then I went upstairs to my babies, bound their wounds, kept them warm and safe." She snickered, but bitterly. "Gave them chicken soup. My babies' last meal was damned chicken soup from a can." Even she was breaking down at this memory, but she inhaled through gritted teeth and kept going.

"I kept them in there for three days, as quiet as I could make them. Nobody else bothered us. Like Sarah, I thought I should have some kind of sign, in case people came by to help us, so I put a sheet out the one window, with 'HELP' written on it in marker. When my babies were asleep, I watched the TV, and I knew what was going to happen to them. We only had a small house. They shared the same room. I couldn't leave one in there when the other . . . turned. So I watched them closely.

"When I thought my daughter was nearly gone, I made her a little bed on the floor of the closet in their room and tucked her in it. When I was sure she was gone, I closed the closet door and shoved the back of the chair up under the door handle to hold it. It was only a couple minutes and that horrible banging started on the closet door. Steady. Like a damn drum. She was tiny, though, and I was pretty sure she couldn't get through. I whispered her name, in case it was really her and she could still hear me, but there was never any voice, just the steady banging.

"My son passed a few hours later, and I closed the door on their room and jammed it with another chair the same way. He was bigger, though, and I worried it wouldn't hold, so I risked making a lot of noise by nailing the door shut. I tried to time the hammering with the banging he was making on the door. I was lucky and none of them came to check it out. I went downstairs and I never went upstairs again.

"I ate, I guess, and stayed alive, but I didn't think anything until Jack and them came to get me later. All I remember was that damn banging."

We'd said what we needed to say, that bizarre mixture of way too much and not nearly enough, but just what was necessary and what the alcohol made possible. I stood up, drunker than I thought, but then I hadn't had anything to drink in months. "You all saved my life," I started. "I couldn't find my family, but I'm glad I found you, and I'll try to never let you down."

It was getting to be one of those sloppy drunk moments, and Jack—either holding up better himself, or wishing to avoid any messy disclosures of his own—was the one to shut it down. He raised his glass and toasted, "To the future."

We finished off what we had in our cups.

"Now let's go sleep the sleep of the just," Jack said. The ladies left the way they had come, arm in arm, propping each other up, and Jack took me back to my little cubicle. It was the kind of evening that you wouldn't ever call fun, but you'd look back on it for the rest of your life and know that it was one of the most important times you'd ever have.

Chapter Five

I AWOKE THE next morning with only the slightest of hangovers, and an overall feeling of well-being, of safety and belonging, that I hadn't had since all this had begun. Not even on the ship.

Although last night's food was about the same as I could've scrounged up on my own, breakfast turned out to be slightly better than I had grown used to. My heart leapt when I saw there were more of the burnt biscuits. I think they were leftover, as they seemed harder and drier than before, but the cooks offset this with their post-apocalyptic version of biscuit gravy: since sausage, bacon, or butter were all out of the question, I had to assume this was some mixture of cooking oil and flour, but it tasted like someone had poured the whole pepper shaker in it, making it a pretty lively addition. The thing they served as coffee was the first hot beverage I'd had since leaving the ship, but it was definitely not Starbucks.

"How you doing?" Jack asked as he came up beside me. "Ready for training this morning?" He shadow-boxed a little, like a great big kid. "Show us your moves? See some of ours?"

"I don't know, Jack," I said, finishing off the coffee, but I went along anyway. I followed him to the second floor, into a

small auditorium. There were windows on the east side, with the blinds open, so it was fairly bright. Several people were on-stage. Jack gestured for me to sit in the audience section first as he went up. I looked around and saw Tanya and sat next to her. She didn't seem unhappy to see me.

"Thanks for the social hour last night," she said, leaning over. "You need that once in a while."

"I know I did. How's training go here?"

"Jack will start with a big group, going over some basics with them, what everyone needs to know, even those who aren't really designated as fighters. It's like karate, only you really work on hitting the other guy in the head, and breaking holds."

"Did you do karate before this?"

"Dance instructor. Taught little girls to dance ballet, tap, and jazz. I don't like karate moves, they seem unnatural to me, but I guess dancing helped me pick them up better than some people do."

Jack was on the stage in front of ten people, taking them through what looked like a karate class. They obviously had learned to do a series of set moves like a kata at the beginning of class, then Jack had paired people up and improvised a sort of zombie sparring: one person played the zombie assailant, while the other went through set counterattacks, mostly blows to the head. The class went on for some time, then Jack dismissed them and came down to us.

"Hey, you guys, we're going to take a break, then it's time for my advanced students. That means you, big gal," he gave Tanya a couple playful punches on the shoulder, then turned to give me a couple. "I don't know about you, tough guy, but we'll see if we can get you to where you don't need us saving your ass anymore. Meet me up there in five, Tanya."

"Don't worry," she said, looking over her shoulder at me as she walked up to the stage, with the hint of a smile. "Me and Popcorn will have him pretty softened up before you get up here."

Some of the beginning class had sat in the auditorium to watch, but I looked around to see who this mysterious Popcorn was. At the far left side of the auditorium was a boy of about nine or ten, and I knew it was him. There was no word to describe him except "feral"—he was wiry, tanned like he never came inside during the day, and his hair looked like it had never been cut; it just flowed off his head in a shaggy mess past his shoulders. He looked like Mowgli's evil twin. Between the very in-shape Tanya and the Wild Child over there, I could well imagine that Jack was going to be thoroughly worked over. I was glad, as I had no formal combat training, and I wasn't looking forward to getting up in front of these people who clearly had been working on it pretty hard for some time.

A kid pushed three homemade dummies out onto the stage: one in the back, and one on each side. They were crudely made, like scarecrows. Tanya stood in the middle. Jack came out from the right side, next to the one dummy. He was padded all over, with gloves and a Kevlar helmet, so much that he looked like the Michelin Man. Even though it wasn't a very good place to hit a zombie, as Tanya's story proved, Jack's crotch was understandably the most cushioned part. This was clearly going to be full contact.

"Batons," he said, and the kid gave Tanya two police batons. She twirled them, as she shook out her legs. "Ready?"

"Ready!"

"Begin!" Jack walked toward her, trying to imitate a zombie's slow, lurching gait.

I still think that most fights don't look like anything special, but Tanya definitely made it look more like Chuck Norris than I ever could. She took two steps toward the dummy in the back as she brought her left hand across to her right hip. With a snarl, she unleashed a backhanded blow with her left baton that sent the dummy's head bouncing across the stage. Just for effect, she shoved the torso to the ground and kicked it.

With a flourish, she brought both batons up to either side as she took four steps across the stage. She gave a shout as she slammed both batons together on either side of the second dummy's head, then she kicked it in the midsection and sent it sprawling.

She turned to face Jack, who had only taken a couple steps. Tanya strode up to him, and raising the baton in her left hand as a feint, she swung with her right, trying to hit him in the side of the head. Jack, moving a bit more dexterously than a normal zombie did, caught her right arm.

Enraged, she brought the left baton down on his forearm to break the hold. He groaned and let go. Then she gave him a backhanded blow with the baton in her left hand, followed by the blow from her right that she had originally intended. He staggered back, and she reversed it—backhanded blow with her right, forehand with the left. She raised both batons, and Jack raised his hands. "That's a takedown," he said, I thought a little weakly. "Finish your last opponent."

The batons clattered on the stage as Tanya threw them aside. She walked up to the last dummy, giving it a backhanded fist across the face with her right hand, then grabbed its head and twisted it 180 degrees. She jerked it up, just for effect, like she was going to tear its head off, then shoved the whole dummy to the floor.

"Good job." Jack said, and Tanya returned to sit next to me. "Popcorn, you're up in five."

"So what's the kid's story?" I asked Tanya.

"He was one of the people trapped in the city at the rescue center downtown. They didn't have a chance. The city was the last place you wanted to be, once it started. It was just a few cops and firemen downtown, so once they saw they were surrounded, they didn't try to make a break for it. They just fought and fought and kept losing ground, with the building full of women and kids. I saw it on the TV; they were broadcasting it from the news helicopter, but there was no one to help them.

"Popcorn and his mom were some of the ones who tried to scatter and get away when it was all over. They ran from the center, down the street, and climbed up on a dumpster. His mom lifted him up so he could reach the bottom of a fire escape, but before she could pull herself up, they got her. He had to watch her get eaten, hear her screams. I guess it's like Sarah said—at least it was quick. You don't know how much more messed up he'd be if it hadn't been quick. He looks so tough now, but you can hear him sometimes at night, crying for her."

"Poor kid," I said, watching him ascend to the stage. You could never get used to hearing these stories of horror and sacrifice as civilization collapsed and individuals tried to save those closest to them.

"He climbed up the fire escape and broke a window to get inside the building. Lucky for him, it led to the balcony of the old downtown theater. The balcony had been closed off for years, condemned by the fire department, so the stairway leading up to it was locked. There was a stairway up to the roof that was blocked off from the main theater, too, and he could go anywhere there without them seeing him or being able to get to him. He lived there for two months before we picked him up."

"I take it he lived on popcorn?"

Tanya laughed a little. "Actually, somebody called him Jujube first, but he didn't like that, and we found that pissing him off isn't the smartest thing you can do. Yeah, he got lucky again in the theater: the stairway to the balcony had been used to store stuff, and there was candy, soda, and popcorn, and he lived on that. He'd climb up to the roof and build a little fire to pop it. He even found a huge box of drink cups: he dragged those up to the roof and put them all over to catch rain water."

"How'd he start a fire?"

"More luck. The theater had some kids' meal deal where you got a toy surprise, and one of them was a little plastic magnifying glass. He'd take the wrappers and cardboard boxes and use the sun to light them with that. That's how we spotted him—the smoke from the fire. God was looking out for that kid."

"You think?" It was just a little surprising, coming from her, after the story she had told last night.

"What, some shit happens and I can't believe in God anymore? I don't know why He took my babies, and I don't know why Popcorn's still here, but that doesn't mean I can't hear his story and know, deep down, that he's here for some reason, and I'm supposed to love him like my own."

I looked at her intently. Coming from someone else, such a profession would've struck me as trite and ignorant. But from her, I knew it was the deepest wisdom. I even hoped that maybe someday I could share it.

"Give him the stilettos," Jack was saying as they prepared for another round. "He likes those." It was hard to see from this far back, but it looked like the assistant gave Popcorn two thin-bladed knives. "Ready?"

Tanya lowered her voice. "When he was in the theater, one of those things managed to climb up on the dumpster and got in."

"Begin!"

Popcorn's arm came down, there was a *thwack*, and the dummy right next to Jack had a knife sticking out of its face. It looked like it was right about where its left eye would be.

"Poor zombie," I said quietly.

Jack didn't like the knife-throwing. "Hey! You may not have killed it, and now you're down to one knife!"

"All I need is one," the kid hissed, turning toward the dummy in the back.

"Yeah," Tanya said, continuing her story of the zombie intruder in the theater, "Popcorn whacked it with a broom, but the broom handle broke without bashing its head in."

Popcorn leaped on the dummy at the back of the stage, planting his feet where its hips would be; he grabbed it by the neck and plunged the knife into its eye. As the dummy fell to one side, he jumped off, turned to the left side of the stage, and crouched.

"So he took the broom handle—it was all pointy where it had broken off—and shoved it in its eye. Before he dumped the body, he lowered down a string and pulled the top of the dumpster open, so they couldn't do that again."

"Smart kid."

If Tanya had made knocking the dummies' heads in look like a scene from a Chuck Norris movie, then Popcorn definitely made it look more like the *Matrix*. With a shriek, he ran at the back wall of the stage, took two steps up it, then launched himself at the dummy on the left side of the stage. He stabbed the knife into the side of its head and knocked it over, then kept stabbing it when it was on the ground.

He got up and faced Jack. Popcorn ran right at him, then at the last moment, he threw his feet forward and slid past Jack, like a runner in baseball. Before Jack could turn around, Popcorn had leapt onto Jack's back, where he was pounding both sides of his head, one with the pommel of the knife, the other with his empty left fist.

"Okay! Okay!" Jack conceded defeat, and the kid jumped off him. Popcorn left the stage and walked out of the auditorium. "Okay, Jonah, you're next," Jack said.

I really didn't want to do this. I had no training. All I had done for the last few weeks was hit, shoot, or stab dead people in the head, with no grace or accuracy. Many of them hadn't even gone down permanently dead, but had just kind of flopped around, twitching, and I was lucky to have gotten away from them. My survival in spite of my ineptitude was as sure a proof of God looking out for me as Popcorn's little plastic magnifying glass and soda cups catching rain water. Oddly, as I walked up to the stage, I realized I had never looked at my situation that way until now, though I also realized how little it would save me from embarrassment in front of all these people.

I was in the middle of the stage. "Okay, Jonah," Jack said, "we'll make it easy for you. Give him a bat."

The kid tossed me an aluminum bat. It felt good in my hands, and it was kind of the ideal weapon for whacking dummies in the head.

"Jack," I said, "I don't know about this. Maybe I should just sit this out."

He laughed at me. It was mostly good-natured, I knew at this point, but there still might have been just a little more posturing. From some time in middle school, you learned that guys couldn't completely get past that. "Come on, Jonah, anybody should be able to kill four zombies with a bat, especially when three of them don't even move. Ready?"

"Ready," I said, with no conviction.

"Begin!"

I had seen from the first two combatants that Tanya's was the only logical sequence: take out the one in the back, the one on the left, then Jack, and finally the one on the right. I turned toward the back, took two steps as I raised the bat, then swung it horizontally and took the dummy's head off. I turned to the left, took three steps, and brought the bat down on the other dummy's head. It was all perfunctory and graceless, but at least I hadn't slipped and fallen, or anything else embarrassing.

I turned to face Jack. "I still don't know about this," I said.

"You're halfway there, just finish it."

I closed the distance with him and brought the bat down. Again acting a little more dexterous than a zombie, Jack raised his arms to defend himself from the blow and grabbed the bat with his left hand. This is what I was afraid would happen, and it was starting to annoy me.

I wrestled with him for the bat, then jerked it out of his

grip, throwing him off balance. Then I shoved the end of the bat into his face. I think it stunned him more than anything, and he took a step back.

Holding the bat with my left had, I reached across with my right to grab his wrist, so he couldn't block or grab. I jerked him forward again to put him off balance, as I raised the bat and brought it down on his right shoulder blade. It was a savage blow, but it only made me want to hit him more, so I gave it to him on top of the helmet next. I was raising the bat for a third time when he yelled, "Okay, enough there, killer! This dummy's down, go get the other."

I let go of him and walked to the last dummy. I brought the bat down on its head.

Jack walked up to me, his helmet off, and put his hand on the bat. "Easy, easy there," he said soothingly.

"I don't . . . I never trained . . . it's just embarrassing. I can do it for real, but not like this."

Jack laughed a little, rubbing his shoulder. "That's kind of the problem; you do it a little *too* real."

"I'm sorry," I said. "I didn't mean to."

"It's okay, really. I should've known, wandering around out there alone, you wouldn't be ready to fight just for practice."

Tanya had walked up to us. "Guys, not in front of the kids," she whispered. "Make it look good."

Jack knew what she meant and said in a louder voice, "Great job, really got me there." He slapped me on the back and looked out at the audience.

I realized then some of the difficulties of joining this new community. Like Popcorn, I'd picked up killing on my own, but it was a private, emotional, and, most of all, shameful ordeal each time. Now I'd have to do it in front of others,

and play at it, and joke about it. It would definitely take some getting used to.

Jack caught up with me later that day. I had gone back to the edge of the river. It was the most enlivening, calming place in our very circumscribed little world. "You okay?" he said calmly.

"Yeah, I don't know what happened."

"Don't worry, I should've guessed before it happened. There are so many things you have to adjust to here, sometimes I forget and do things out of order. Usually it goes the other way. We had so many people here at first who had never hit anyone before in anger. What were we supposed to do with them? There weren't enough of us with training and weapons to protect the place, let alone go out and try to forage for supplies.

"And it's not like when you're a kid, and some jerk gets tired of you being afraid of water, so he throws you into the deep end of the pool and yells, 'Sink or swim!' We couldn't open the gates and shove people out there and yell, 'Kill them before they eat you!' So we trained them. Katas, sparring, dummies—we got them to pretend to hit things. We got them to get good at pretending to be good at hitting things.

"But it was just pretend. And the first time they went out to defend the gates, or on a raid to scrounge up supplies, they usually froze. And crapped their pants. And then, if they managed to pull it together and bash some stiff's head in, and they had brains splattered all over themselves, they usually stopped to puke. And hopefully they didn't get themselves killed. But sometimes they did. And sometimes the guy next to them, too.

A lot of times they came back bitten and sick. And guess who had to sit up with them? And when they turned, guess who had to split their skull with an axe, so we could save a bullet?" He stopped and shook his head.

"But you're different," he continued. "You've gotten okay at killing. Not great, but you're definitely not going to freeze if one of those things comes up out of the water right now. But you don't like practicing it. It's not pretend for you: it's *too* real for you, it's *too* personal, and you can't pretend. I'm sorry. I should've guessed, but Popcorn was one of the few people we picked up that was like that. Tanya was a little, too. But they were both eager to practice, so they could get better and kill as many of those things as possible. They have a lot of rage that you don't. You're just resigned to it. And that's good. I respect that. And it'll work good here. I think I have enough hot heads and enough people who are too scared. So don't worry, Jonah."

"Thanks, Jack."

"Anyway, since we had so much trouble training people right for combat, that was one of the things Milton thought to change when he arrived. He wanted an initiation rite, I guess you'd call it."

"Sounds a little bizarre."

"Well, don't be too quick. People need rituals, they need some kind of structure or plan, and most of the old ones are gone. We don't have to go to church, or school, or work. We can't vote, or pay taxes, or take tests to get driver's licenses or black belts or whatever. It puts people too much up in the air, and then they get in trouble, either in here with one another, or out there when they're fighting."

"I guess so." Again, the subtler points of the new society were constantly eluding me, but I was trying to adapt.

"So we started making rules, and getting them accepted by the group. Some were straightforward, like you've seen: no weapons, no hoarding food, no stealing, hands off anybody else's man or woman. The usual Ten Commandments stuff. Rules for sanitation and for dealing with infected people. Rules for settling disputes. But once we had those, Milton still thought there had to be something more, something other than prohibitions. Responsibilities, something that made us a community and not just a bunch of people who still had a pulse and had ended up at the same place. So we started having two levels of citizenship. First, if you're part of the community, then you work. You do whatever you're good at it, and we all take turns with the jobs nobody wants. If you don't work, you don't eat. We'd already pretty much been doing that, but we made sure it was a rule, and everybody agreed to it."

"Makes sense."

"Then we had the trickier one, the one that would involve an initiation rite. We decided that anybody could stay here and be protected, so long as they did some kind of work, but they couldn't be full citizens and participate in making the group's decisions unless they fought. If you don't fight, you don't vote."

"Seems kind of harsh."

"I thought so too, but I was surprised how little fuss there was over it. Everyone seemed to like it, even if it meant they wouldn't vote. Like Sarah—she'll never try to get citizenship, and she thinks it's fair that way. I guess the idea of having less responsibility but less rights, or more rights and more responsibility, just made sense to most people. So we've been doing it that way since."

"And this initiation rite?"

"We didn't know what to do exactly. I mean, in the regular

world, I guess these things just developed over time; you didn't sit down and make them up. We didn't know whether to make it just symbolic, you know, like being knighted with a sword. People actually didn't seem to like that. They wanted it to be some kind of real, first act of fighting that would initiate you as a warrior and a citizen. But we had to be practical: there wasn't any sense in fighting and risking your life unless there was something more than a symbolic payoff. We wanted it to yield some real benefit for the group, as well as initiating the person.

"So for our 'citizenship test,' we've been sending people out in little groups, without guns, to raid the city for 'special,' non-essential supplies. We go out in force to get the food and fuel, but everybody looks forward to initiation days, because they'll bring back a few little things that make us more human and remind us of what we've got to fight our way back to—soap, CDs, pens and paper. The remnants of civilization, I guess you'd call them. When a group of three or four new people has trained enough that they think they're ready, then we send them out."

"How many come back?"

"All of them. They have something to work for, they're not rushed into anything, and they're ready. And they have a walkie-talkie: if they call for help, we go get them. They just don't get citizenship then. I've lost people on regular raids, but not on initiations."

"And you want me to do this, I take it?"

"Maybe someday. I was just telling you the kinds of things Milton has thought of, and how we live here, because I guess it must be strange, just being thrust into it. I think you should go meet him now. It's always an interesting conversation."

"Yes, that sounds good. A lot better than the practice fighting."

He smiled. "You like the water, don't you?"

"Yeah, I do. Sometimes I forget how much. I guess that's why I always liked working on the ships. I missed my family, but it was a good time to recharge and regroup."

"Yeah, I used to like to go fishing in a rowboat with my dad when I was little. Didn't do it so much when I grew up. Maybe that's why I was never regrouped enough." He looked thoughtful and smiled. "Well, Jonah, I hope someday you and I can get on a boat and do some fishing. But until then, let's take you to see Milton. I think you'll find he kind of recharges you in a way, too. Definitely always gets me thinking."

Chapter Six

I FOLLOWED JACK to the third floor of the museum, to the end of the corridor where a glass door was labeled "LIBRARY." The room was on a corner of the library, with windows on two sides, and therefore very brightly lit. Wherever there weren't windows, bookcases were built into the walls, and these were full. There were several tables and chairs for studying in the room. Milton was sitting in a comfortable chair, reading, and he rose to greet me.

He was in late middle age, I'd guess in his mid fifties. He was as tall as Jack, but looked like he had always been slim, even before a life of privation. He was dressed in some sort of baggy pants, and a covering like a poncho or smock on top of them: it was really just a big piece of fabric with a hole cut out for his head, drawn tight around his waist with a piece of rope. His hair and beard were completely white, but not as unkempt as most people's.

Overall, he was perhaps the only person I'd met since the end of the world who I would say looked dignified, but he was not especially imposing or mysterious-looking. I guess I had expected Yoda and had gotten Obi Wan.

Milton extended his hand in greeting. He wore wire-rimmed

granny glasses, and I had to keep myself from smiling; the only celebrities I could remember wearing those were John Lennon and Heinrich Himmler: though I suppose both had some claim to charisma, neither was a particularly striking or intimidating looking man, and neither was Milton.

In a way, he too was somehow appropriate to our particular apocalypse. The world had ended in such a mundane way, with your utterly ordinary neighbors attacking you and turning you into yet another member of a mindless, anonymous mob. So maybe it made a sort of sense that the new leader or prophet of the apocalypse would be an entirely regular-looking man.

But then I thought of Tanya and her steadfast love of God and Popcorn, deeper than any theologian's, and her Stoical acceptance of her children's horrible deaths, as strong as any Greek philosopher's or Roman statesman's, and I knew there needn't be anything aristocratic or exotic about wisdom. Milton was what he was, and if he had brought some guidance to this community, then I had better respect that.

"Jonah Caine," Milton said happily. He paused a moment, then added, "We have all killed many of our brothers, haven't we?"

"Yes, unfortunately, we have," I said, not knowing where else to go with his reference to my name.

Jack spoke up. "Milton, I'll leave you two alone for a bit. I have some things to do."

"Yes, thank you, Jack," Milton said amiably. "Amiable" was a good word for him. He just seemed easy-going, more than guru-like.

As we sat there, I caught a whiff of something foul. It was the odor we had all grown used to in the last year—the smell of decay and rot, of gangrenous infection and lingering death. The windows to the room were all open, and a breeze was blowing through, but I didn't think it was from outside. We were too high up, and the direction of the wind wasn't right for it to be blowing around from the front, where we had fought and incinerated so many zombies the day before, and it wasn't a burnt smell, either. In fact, I thought the windows were left open to air the place out and get rid of the smell.

Milton noticed my discomfiture. "I'm sorry, Mr. Caine, it's part of my . . . condition. I'll explain more later, if that's all right."

"Oh, of course," I said, embarrassed, "I didn't mean anything. And call me Jonah, if you want." I suddenly wondered whether everyone was on a first- or last-name basis with Milton, but this wasn't the time to ask.

He smiled. "Thank you. Tell me how you came to us."

I repeated my story more or less as I had told it the night before, though more briefly and matter-of-factly in this setting. Milton watched and listened as though it was imperative to note every nuance and detail and word choice. When I finished speaking, he leaned back and looked off dreamily, seeming to digest everything I'd said, when, of course, the whole story was quite straightforward and uninteresting to me.

"You're so lucky," he finally said. "You must've read so many books as an English professor."

I was taken aback, to say the least. Jack would've asked me about the details of killing zombies or how I survived, Tanya would've asked about my family, and Sarah, well, she probably would've just cried. But Milton was the only person I could imagine who would've been interested in what it was like to be a damned English professor at a community college. It was hard for me to understand, but again, it seemed to fit him.

"Well, yes," I said, "I suppose I did. I always liked reading. I mean, I used to. Not so much anymore."

"I hope you reacquire the habit someday. Let's go over by the window. It should make the smell more tolerable for you as well." He got up and walked past the bookshelves. "I never read books before coming here. But once I was here, it was all I wanted to do."

He looked at me intently again. "You see, there were all these people here, and they seemed automatically to look up to me, like I was a messiah sent to save them. But I'm not, Jonah, and I keep telling them that, but it doesn't seem to sink in. I'm glad I can talk to you because I doubt you'll have that misconception. But they did, right away, once they saw my . . . condition."

He paused just a moment, looking at his hands. I now noticed they were mottled, like with liver spots on old people, but these were light-gray patches. I still wasn't sure why the people here longed for a smelly messiah with weird eczema, but I was eager to find out.

Milton continued, more calmly again. "Anyway, I was with all these people here, and they seemed to need me to lead them, guide them, help them. And I didn't have a clue what to do for them. So I wanted to read books, maybe get some ideas." He gestured to the shelves. "Most everything here was about science, or nineteenth century local history. That's not what I needed, though a few books on psychology were useful, as were some on the hardships faced by settlers here, and on the wisdom of the Native Americans.

"Fortunately, the traveling exhibition downstairs was on Ancient Rome, so they had a few books on history, literature, politics, philosophy, mythology, religion: that's what I needed.

"And one time when Jack went out foraging for food, I

begged him to take me along, so I could get more books. I didn't want to risk anyone else hunting around for books, so I would do it myself, but I had to have more books. Jack looked at me like I was crazy, but even he thinks I have some gift, so he humored me. I needed books on what makes people tick, on what they value, on how they get along with each other. So I read, and I learned. And with Jack's help, we built up the community."

The story was more preposterous than I ever could've imagined. If the guy could perform telekinesis or levitate, it would've made more sense to me. If he was just some glib, charismatic, fast talker who had conned everyone, that would really make sense. I'd hate him for it, but it would make sense at least. But a reluctant messiah who educated himself with books looted from the local Barnes and Noble—it really seemed comical.

Still, I had to admit that, unlike all the religious and political hucksters who had run a con before the dead rose, at least Milton had never taken any money from anyone; he hadn't gotten some revelation that he should be surrounded by a harem and fed grapes, and he seemed quite eager to debunk himself.

So, again, if it worked for this community that I wanted to be a part of, it seemed silly to look down on or ridicule them. But I did want a little more proof of profundity before I embarked on an initiation rite that involved running around, unarmed, among the hungry dead, looking for Air Wicks and silk flowers, or whatever it was I was going to be doing.

"What, exactly, did you learn?" I asked, and it came out a little more accusatorily than intended.

"Jonah, I learned about human nature, which I have to say, I had never once considered before coming here. I don't think many people do. Reading all those wonderful books, I am sure you thought about it before, didn't you?"

He was so simple that it was wonderfully disarming. I still didn't quite understand what the people here thought was so miraculous about him, but I did see how they could come to him with their problems and respect his answers. It was impossible to imagine him being arrogant or selfish or forcing his opinion on someone.

"Yes, I did," I replied. "I'm not sure I came to any conclusions, though."

He laughed for the first time, and it was even more disarming than his little, ingenuous questions. "Good! I couldn't very well talk to you if you had, because I know I don't have answers, only questions, and you'd be quite bored with how stupid I must seem. But if you have questions, too, then maybe we can ask some together. Or does Jack have some eminently practical, necessary thing for you to do? Dig a ditch or build a wall or kill something? He loves that kind of thing so much, it's funny."

"No, no, he didn't mention anything."

"Wonderful!" He leaned back and looked off dreamily again, his own thousand yard stare. I could see that Milton was pretty much *all* thousand yard stares, and it was nice to see someone enjoying them for a change.

"I think the thing that surprised and interested me the most was how so many people agree that people's souls have several parts. They differ on what to call them, or how many there are, but they agree that there are parts. Had you always known that there were several parts? I found it so amazing!"

Again, his innocence was quite captivating, and also, as Jack had said, energizing, either to someone who hadn't considered the things he was talking about, or to someone like me, who had thought of them too much, in the desiccated, constipated way that academics or experts do. "Well, Milton, I don't think I had been raised to believe that, but I do remember learning it in college, and I remember it was exciting to me then."

"Yes, that's what I mean! What a marvelous life you had, to learn such an important thing so young. It made it so much easier for me to see how people would interact here, or what they would need. Look at Jack: can you think of someone who's more the embodiment of the rational part of the soul? All his plans and schemes and calculations!"

I smiled. "Yes, I think that's his part of the soul, Milton."

"So I know when I talk to Jack, it has to be all logic and business. But he knows now that sometimes he leaves people's emotions out of his calculations, and now we work much better together. For instance, did he tell you about burying the bodies?"

"Yes, he said you did that for the people here, but not for those you killed."

"Yes, but even before I got here, people had argued with him about what to do with the bodies. He wanted to dump them all over the back wall and be done with it. He said we couldn't afford the calories we'd spend digging holes for them, and we didn't have the fuel to burn them. He would compromise, grudgingly, but once I could understand what was going on, how he was looking at it differently, it made more sense to me, and we could discuss it."

He paused just a moment, and I could guess he was switching gears. "And while we're discussing that—tell me, if it's all right, why did you go looking for your family?"

That question took me by surprise again. I was trying to tie it in with his observations on human nature, but then I thought that I should just answer it as straightforwardly as possible. "Because I loved them and missed them?"

"Yes, I know, but I wonder if there was something more going on. You don't think, for example, that you loved them more than all the thousands of people who didn't go looking for their loved ones, who just assumed, once it all started, that they were dead and there was no point?"

"No, no, I don't remember ever thinking that I loved them more than other people loved their families."

"And I believe you were right not to think that. And please don't think I mean that you didn't love them, but it just seems to me that it also has to do with your will being the predominant part of your soul. Once you made a decision, a commitment, then the logic or the emotion involved were really beside the point. You went alone across hundreds of miles with literally millions of walking corpses all around, because you thought it was your responsibility. It was quite remarkable, too. I don't think Jack could've done it, even with all his training. Or Tanya—I don't think she could carry on like that for so long, though think of how much explosive power she has at any given moment. You've seen her fight?"

"Yes."

"It's amazing, isn't it? And a little frightening, to have so much rage. If you were being attacked, hand to hand, who would you want fighting alongside you?"

"Tanya—pure, raw emotion."

"Exactly. Each part has its uses, has a place to fit, and has its own people devoted especially to it."

"And which one is the most important?"

His eyes really sparkled, and he smiled. "Oh, I am so glad you came here! No one here would think to ask me that!

They just let me ramble on, and they're so convinced I've been touched by God or some such thing that we never just *talk*! I have to say, I haven't yet read anything that I agree with about that question. I really don't see how you could say one part is better, or more important."

"And which one are you?"

He laughed again. "Oh, my, now a question like that would really not be asked by anyone else here! But so much more fun! I have to be honest and say I'm not sure. It's not a cop-out: I'm really not sure. I definitely have no will at all. Look at how I just went along with being their leader, even though it's the thing I least want! I have some reason, surely, but not like Jack. And nothing like Tanya's emotions. Again, it would surprise the people here, but I'm afraid I'm pretty average."

He had me so intrigued and enthralled by such an abstract conversation. I'd say I hadn't had one like that in months, but really, it had been long before the dead rose since I could talk to someone like this, probably all the way back to my days as a student. "And what about the flesh, our bodies? A lot of religions and philosophies make a lot of that, or say we've made too much of it."

He shook his head. "That's another one where I'm not sure anyone I've read has it completely right. But there is something wrong with the flesh, isn't there? I mean, isn't that what this is all about?" He gestured toward the window. "Look at them out there. Have you ever really looked at them—closely?"

I remembered the girl in the convenience store, and Daniel Gerard, and the little boy outside the gates, and I shuddered. And that wasn't even one day's worth of carnage at my hands. "Yes, I have. And I can't stand it."

Milton nodded. "I thought you had, and there again you

see how we're each different. Jack can slice them open or blow them up or set them on fire, all without blinking an eye, because it just makes sense to do so, like cutting off a wart. Tanya can do it because she's so angry at them. Either one could be knee-deep in gore, and it'd be like rain drops off a goose.

"But if you don't have either of those two reactions, the walking dead are most disturbing, aren't they? They're flesh all by itself—without reason, or emotion, or even will—simple, unguided, unadorned. Just flesh that won't lie down and die and go back into the earth. And, I have to admit, it is the flesh that causes me a good deal of pain and inconvenience, and gives the people here all their overblown opinions of me."

I paused, but the suspense was getting to me. "I'm afraid I don't understand, and maybe it's none of my business, but why do they think all these things about you and your . . . condition?"

He sighed. "Yes, I have to tell you, before you get some crazy, embellished version from someone else here. Please don't expect anything too exciting. It's just another story of coincidences and luck that brought me here, signifying nothing."

I smiled. "Well, I think now that at least it's not being told by an idiot."

He laughed harder than before. "Oh my, that is good! I should've known not to drop Shakespeare references with an English professor, but that one really slipped out without my remembering where it was from! I am so going to like having you here!"

Milton finally began his story. He had been a scientist before the dead rose. It was completely illogical, but I think, like anyone, I had to ask, "You weren't, you know, involved with . . . what happened?"

"Oh my, no! I worked in biotech, but nothing that was related to what happened. It was just cancer research."

I smiled grimly. "Funny to call it 'just' cancer research, like it was some minor thing you were trying to fix."

He nodded and smiled back, less grimly than I. "Yes, I suppose it is." He shook his head as he told me how he had survived when the crisis had first unfolded. "I was a terrible coward, Jonah. I've told everyone that, too. I just cowered in my townhouse, with everything barricaded as best I could, and I didn't make a sound."

His wife had been on a business trip at the time and was almost certainly dead. For his daughter he had a little more hope. "She had been on a camping trip. Maybe she was far enough out in the wilderness that she might have survived. I like to think so, but I wasn't like you. I couldn't just walk across the country, looking for her. No, I just hid."

Like thousands of people in the same situation—exactly like Sarah, Tanya, and I had done at the beginning—Milton had sat and watched things unfold on the television till the power went off. Then he just sat in the dark—until his cell phone rang.

"It was some government agency," he said. "It was almost as scary as what was going on out in the street, the fact there was a list somewhere of anyone who worked in biotech. But there must've been one, and they'd worked their way down to me. They must've been desperate to be calling someone whose work was totally unrelated to weapons research or epidemiology, but I guess by the time they thought to research what was happening, most everyone with any applicable knowledge was already dead, or walking around without a functioning brain. So at that point they were just trying to find anyone with a Ph.D. or an M.D."

Milton told whoever it was on the phone that he was in his townhouse. The caller informed him that they would be there any second and that he should get ready by the front door. A few minutes later, Milton saw a helicopter hovering over his front yard, with two soldiers sliding down ropes.

They took him to a military airbase, but the undead had already overrun it. They were all over the runway, and the pilot nearly gave up at that point. "But the commander of the group was more calm and in command of the situation," Milton said. "He pointed at a big transport jet that some soldiers were defending, and he told the pilot just to land next to it for a few seconds, then he'd be on his own if he wanted."

The soldiers on the ground formed a ring around the ramp in the back of the plane, shooting, trying to hold back the dead till the group from the helicopter could get on board and take off. The plane was loaded with soldiers, some civilians, and piles of crates and supplies. They flew for a long time, and finally set down at an airstrip in the Rocky Mountains.

Milton smiled, recalling his own naiveté about the area. "I was so surprised to see snow on the highest peaks. I'd always heard of such places in the West, but I'd never bothered to travel. I guess I picked the worst possible time to start.

"When we got off the plane, I could see we were in a place where there weren't any zombies around. But when I looked at the cyclone fence in the distance, I could see shapes crowded there, and I knew what they were. They were everywhere, not just in the cities or on the east coast. We were so isolated there weren't enough at the fence to threaten us, but I knew then there really wasn't any escape from them."

Their group consisted of five scientists and a dozen soldiers. Since they'd been assembled so haphazardly and with no real organization, there wasn't much they could do. "We didn't have any plan, or any way to direct our work, especially since we didn't even work in the same fields. And the supplies were just a random assortment of lab equipment. Every time someone had any kind of an idea that might go somewhere, we had to abandon it because we didn't have the right equipment or supplies."

With such meager resources, they did little other than confirm what everyone already knew—that it was a virus spread by bites. With nothing useful to do, they puttered through the summer and early fall.

"All we really wanted to do was just sit back and enjoy what time we had," Milton said with that dreamy, wistful look of his. "The base was in a breathtaking caldera, one of the most beautiful places I'd ever seen. A spring bubbled up in the midst of the camp. I'd never seen water just bubble up from the ground before; it looked like something in a storybook. There were flowers everywhere. It made me remember that, when I was little, my mother and I would pick wild strawberries in fields sometimes. I guess we were at the caldera too late in the summer because I didn't see any, but I bet there are some there now.

"Every day, I'd wish that we could just plant some crops and stay there. And I'd wish that there were some women in the group, if not for me, then at least to give us some hope of survival for the group in that paradise."

Slowly, it became clear that they couldn't stay there. Their food would eventually run out. The jet barely had any fuel, and they didn't know where to fly anyway. But they did have two old jeeps on the base, and they knew of other facilities like theirs nearby. Initially, they'd been in communication with them, though by the autumn, they hadn't heard from anyone in weeks.

The nearest base was about thirty miles away, and apparently, it was a much larger one. They thought maybe it would have more supplies, so they decided to check it out. Milton went with two soldiers in a jeep.

"There were no zombies at their fence," Milton said, much quieter now, not as animated. "The gate was still locked, but we'd brought bolt cutters for just such a situation.

"Everything was deserted, silent, still. I'm sure you know, Jonah, being out there alone for so long, sometimes the loneliness and desperation make you get so optimistic that it just seems crazy. As I talk about it now, I know we should've run the minute we got there. A completely deserted compound, where we knew there had been dozens of armed men? How could we possibly hope to find something *good*?

"But we kept thinking maybe they had left the place, and maybe there were still some supplies there, and we could just grab them and go. Maybe it really was a good thing that they weren't still there, or they might not want to share with us. We'd tell each other such nonsense as we went from empty room to empty room."

He paused again, and this time he bowed his head and rubbed his eyes. "I'm sorry," he said quietly. "I told you, I'm such a little coward. I should be able to tell a simple story without getting all emotional. You'll have to give me a minute." He shuddered. He was shaking. "It was most definitely *not* a good thing that there were no people left there. No, no, *not* a good thing at all."

Chapter Seven

THEY FOUND THE labs in the compound, which were more damaged than the other rooms, with splotches on the floor of what looked like dried blood. The labs contained cages of various sizes, all empty. In one of the larger labs, they found all the equipment smashed and scattered all over the floor, and more empty cages all over. Some of the cages looked like the bars had been ripped apart. Puddles and smears of blood had dried everywhere.

They finally decided they'd seen enough and it was time to retreat. "We turned back to the door to the smaller lab, and then we saw them to our right," Milton said, very quiet at this point of the story. "I guess our eyes had adjusted enough to see in the gloom, or they had stepped forward from the deeper shadows in the back of the lab. Three big dogs. Their fur and skin were torn off in spots, matted with blood. And they had those eyes, you know, like the dead have, all cloudy."

"How could they?" I asked. "The infection has never affected animals."

"I know, that's what we said, but it didn't make any difference. The scientists must've been working on a different strain of the virus at that facility. Or they created it by mistake. I don't know. But the dogs were definitely standing there, and they definitely weren't alive.

"The ranking soldier whispered to back slowly toward the door. As we did, he shoved his .45 in my hand. He told me, 'Do what you can, Doc. I'm sorry we got you into this.' I told him I wouldn't be any better off still cowering in my townhouse, and he just nodded."

The three of them edged toward the door. The soldier who gave Milton his .45 was the same one who had made the pilot land next to the jet back at the airbase. I smiled at how kind and grateful Milton sounded when he described such bravery. I guess, like Jack or Tanya, things had hardened and calloused me more, and I haven't appreciated such little things as another person's bravery. That's where Milton seems to have survived better than many of the rest of us: he can still see the moments of grace and virtue amidst the horror.

But the horror in the lab had continued. The other soldier couldn't take the pressure and ran for the door. Apparently, zombie dogs—if, God forbid, there are more such abominations out there—aren't as slow as zombie humans, and they were all over him. Milton and the commanding soldier started shooting, but in the dark, they weren't too accurate. They probably hit the soldier more than once before they finally put down the dogs.

They went to drag the wounded man out. "But then we heard scraping noises in the main lab, and we saw them." Again, his voice dropped lower. "Monkeys, dogs, cats, even smaller animals like rabbits and rats—all their lab animals, undead, edging toward us. And in the smaller lab, some of the undead scientists and soldiers were staggering toward us. I thought for sure we were finished.

"The commander took the wounded man's submachine gun, so he had one in each hand. He whispered to me, 'Doc, try to take out the human zombies in there. They're bigger targets, you might get lucky. These killer bunnies and shit are going to be the real problem. Damn things have brains about the size of a damn walnut.'

"We started shooting again. It seemed like it went on for hours, though it must've been only a few seconds. We shot until we were out of bullets, then we fought them hand to hand. I'm sure you know—the .45 is a big, ugly piece of iron in your hand, and I did the best I could with it, bashing them in the head. In the end, we put them all down, but we were bitten up by the animals, so it was only a matter of time before it was all over. The soldier who'd first been attacked by the dogs was already dead. The commander took the .45 from me, reloaded it, and finished him when he got back up. He had the decency to say, 'God forgive me,' as he did it. People's decency has also constantly amazed me in all this, Jonah. He told me to do the same for him when it came time, if he went first, and to be sure to save a bullet for myself."

But the attack hadn't killed them, and even though they thought that death was inevitable, the will to survive almost never listens to rational thought or logical analysis—it just fights and scraps. In that sense, the zombies are just exaggerations of what we always do—fight to live, whether we should or not. So the two survivors searched and found bandages, and Milton dressed their wounds as best he could. They took shelter in a different building and found some food.

"We even boiled some water with a Bunsen burner and had tea." Milton laughed and shook his head. "Sipping tea right next to a damn slaughterhouse, with poison coursing through our veins—what were we thinking? But on the other hand—why not?

"It hurt like crazy, of course. Burning, wracking pain, with fever and shaking. We took turns, only one of us sleeping at a time, so the other could shoot him in case he turned. We didn't know what to do if the guy who was awake turned while the other one slept, but we didn't have a better plan.

"After a couple days, we actually seemed to be improving. You know how most people are gone in hours, unless it's just a scratch, and we were both bitten all over. After a week, it seemed as though, so long as you didn't die from loss of blood, the infection from the animal strain wouldn't kill you. I don't know whether the virus had just mutated again, or if this strain the animals had contracted had always been that way, and the people originally on the base had all bled to death, and that's how they became zombies. I still have no idea why we survived.

"But a definite downside was that the pain didn't go away. It was like it had become a low-grade infection, and it would always hurt—forever. It makes it difficult and painful to breathe or move. At least it has for me, ever since. And sleeping—you can just about forget about sleeping. And then we noticed the smell. I mean, we noticed it at first, but we thought it was because we were dying. But it never went away. It's like the rot and death are inside us, never healing, but never quite finishing us off."

The two of them had gathered up some food and headed back to their own base. When they got there, Milton had taken the .45 and the commander had gotten out a shovel, so they could kill the zombies at the gate and get inside. "But that's when we noticed their reaction to us.

"As soon as we got out of the jeep, when we must've

still been about fifteen or twenty feet away from them, they all started to cower, with their hands up to their faces, like we were really bright lights that were blinding them. The commander motioned for me not to shoot. We walked toward them, and they started to back away from us. We could just shoo them away from the gate. It was like in the cartoons, when an elephant is stomping everything in sight, and then it sees a mouse and runs away. We were thrilled. Now we could gather food or anything else and bring it back to the camp.

"But when we went in, we found that everyone else had left. The other jeep was gone. They must have waited a couple days, and when we didn't come back, they gave up and went their own way. We waited a couple days to see if they'd come back, and to enjoy our mountain paradise a little longer, then we split up and went our separate ways, to look for them, or any other human survivors that we could help with our new gift."

He'd wandered for weeks before he found the museum. He was lucky, as it was starting to get cold by then, and Milton freely admitted he lacked any kind of outdoors skills to survive in the wilderness on his own, even if he was safe from the undead.

"When the people here saw my gift," he said, smiling, "they thought I was their salvation, and I could do anything. I tried to explain that it was just some wild, unforeseeable side effect of a mutant virus, but I heard them whisper—that I'm sent from God, and I can kill zombies by looking at them, and if you touch me then a zombie can't bite you for twenty-four hours. I can't do all that crazy stuff. I really can't do that much of anything. Sometimes the pain is too intense for me to go out and gather supplies or help people. And even when I do, I can't carry everything by myself, so we still have to risk other people on our raids. And I can't protect them. It's not like I have mind control over the zombies—they just avoid me.

"I assume it's because of some smell, maybe pheromones. They think I'm one of them, maybe even some kind of alpha or king zombie, though God forbid I could be something so horrible as that. But unless someone is pressed up against me, I can't keep the dead from attacking them. I do what I can, and we've lost very few people since I came here, I'm proud to say. My pain is a little price to pay to help build up this community."

He sighed and leaned back. "That's my story, Jonah. I'm sorry it took so long to tell, and I'm sorry I got so worked up, when others have been through so much worse."

"No," I said, "it's amazing. I know you don't like to hear it, but it really does seem like your coming here was a miracle for these people. And since they saved me, now it's a miracle for me, too."

He smiled. "Oh no, not you, too! Aren't there real miracles all around us? Isn't that enough? Why do people look at one thing rather than another and put all the pressure and stigma of 'miracle' on it? It's a miracle the people here survived for months before I got here, or there wouldn't have been anything for me to 'save,' and I probably would've frozen to death during the winter. No one is really a savior, I don't think. I think we just help each other. Or, we're supposed to."

We sat, just staring out the window. It was another beautiful spring day, and I was feeling quite content, even pleased, with Milton's way of looking at things.

Milton broke the silence again after a moment. "Isn't it wonderful that the place they could seal off and defend was a museum? I just assumed, as I wandered around, that I'd find survivors at an army base, or storage facility, or some other place with nothing but concrete walls and barbed wire and fluorescent lighting. But instead, we're here, surrounded by so many beautiful and amazing things, things we can use to teach the children about how life was, and to remind us that life isn't just canned food to eat and a wall to keep you from being eaten. It keeps us from becoming merely animals, I think."

"Yes, I've been thinking that as I looked around here. It was very fortunate."

"Another of your miracles, I suppose?" He smiled. "Maybe so. Maybe, somehow, events conspired to make sure we had just a little more than the barest of necessities. And now I think we need to work on getting more such things, just as much as we need food and other supplies."

"Jack told me about your initiation rite, that you use it as an opportunity to get such non-essentials."

"And what do you think of such a task?"

"I was skeptical at first, to be honest."

He nodded. "I can imagine. I think you have to be a part of the group for it to make sense. I'm sorry you weren't here when we started it."

"Yes, I think that's what I'm realizing. But I think I can see its value. And if you have Jack sold on the idea, then it can't be totally unreasonable, can it?"

He smiled. "Quite right, though he had to be convinced to see its value, just like with burying the bodies. But anyone can see, I think, that people need more than just food and shelter. Allow not nature more than nature needs . . ."

"Man's life is cheap as beast's," I finished the quotation.

Milton laughed. "Now that time I was being just a little naughty and trying to catch you. Do you know I hadn't read Shakespeare since high school, before I came here? And the only play I remembered from high school was *Macbeth*. Witches and ghosts and bloodstained hands—all quite appropriate to how we live now, I suppose. But now I'm amazed at what else I've read in his plays."

He looked up again with his dreamy look. "Isn't that strange—we had all his plays, just sitting around, and I never bothered to read them? And now we have to fight and kill to get some copies of his books and others, books that are blowing around at the smashed-up local bookstore, quickly turning into dust. Maybe that was what was wrong with the way we used to live—so many luxuries sitting around that we didn't appreciate them."

"Too many, and the wrong kind."

"Exactly. I think we should have to work for luxuries and not just be handed them." He gave a mischievous little grin. "Well, there was one time when I thought the people here just needed to be handed some luxuries and shouldn't have to fight for them."

"Oh, when was that?"

"I hardly think it'd be considered too indulgent. We had a long, wet fall last year. By December, everything was all muddy and gross, but not really cold."

"Global warming? I wish that was all we had to worry about anymore."

"Yes. My point is, everyone was feeling down. So I snuck out one night. I'm sure Jack would've blamed me for wasting batteries and risking getting hurt, but I had to try. I didn't know

my way around that well because I had been too sick to go on many of the raids, but I did find what was left of one big store. The dead seemed especially docile that night, parting before me as I invaded their little castle or tomb. They didn't seem to cringe from me so much as bow and scrape. I know it's crazy, but maybe even they can be made to feel peaceful, under the right circumstances. I filled a huge sack with various things and dragged it back here. We didn't have a bad Christmas, all things considered."

I smiled. Milton had again lapsed into painting a rather absurd image, a Santa trudging through walking corpses to bring back a bag of goodies from the remnants of Wal-Mart. But again, in a world of unrelenting ugliness and brutality, it had a certain charm, a kind of humble beauty and value that you couldn't ignore.

"But other than that one night, I think perhaps we got too spoiled in our old world, and I wanted a world where we'd have beauty, but we'd appreciate it better, not take it for granted. So I wanted to work it into the initiation, the thing that made people ready to enter the community, by having them show that they could fight and struggle and present everyone with something that wasn't just useful, but beautiful or uplifting, even if it was just in some tiny little way. Maybe *especially* if it was only a tiny little thing! God, do you remember how pretty women's toes used to look with nail polish on them, wearing sandals in the summer? Now *that* was something!"

I laughed and shook my head. So did Milton, and for a long time. "Oh my God, Milton, now how did you go from Shakespeare to toenail polish as the essence of what makes us human and separates us from the beasts or zombies!"

"I'm sorry, I'm sorry. I told you I haven't had anyone to

talk to, and it all just comes spilling out now. But really," he turned serious again, "I hope that some day we have the place built up enough that we can just take the food and safety for granted, and people can start to work on their own for better things, whatever it is that excites them, whether it's cosmetics or Shakespeare or disco. Wouldn't that be something? To have the luxury again of people being poets, or musicians, or fashion designers, or athletes? Don't you want that for your children? And is it so much to ask?" He got a little quieter. "Did we mess up so bad that our children don't even deserve *that*?"

Talking to him was like careening down a twisting road, and he'd made the next curve and was on to his next phase, or his next role. Now he wasn't the reluctant messiah, or the guy infected with a mutant virus that allowed him to defeat the living dead, or a post-apocalyptic Santa with a toe fetish: now I could see a glimpse of how he could motivate people to organize politically, to have an agenda and make sacrifices to accomplish something and become part of something greater than themselves. I don't think Milton was all the way to an "Ask not what your country can do for you" speech, or an "I have a dream" speech, but he was miles ahead of the "No child left behind," or "I feel your pain" kind of rhetoric to which we'd become so debased and accustomed.

"I think you'll be able to pull that off here, Milton, maybe sooner rather than later."

"I hope you're right, Jonah. And I hope you'll help us."

"Oh, I'm sure I will. You and Jack just let me stay here a little longer before you send me back out there. I've been among the dead too long. Now I'd like to enjoy life here a little. I've been dying to live, I guess you could say."

Milton smiled and rose. "Not my best pronouncement,

I hope, but it seemed right as a slogan for people to come in and rest."

"It worked for me," I said as we shook hands.

"I'm so glad it did," Milton said. He led me to the door, and we parted for the day.

Chapter Eight

A FEW WEEKS passed. I moved from my guest room to the main living quarters. I got used to fighting practice with Jack and Tanya in the mornings, and I got to where I could fight without getting all worked up, finally moving with some grace and ease. When I was done there, I'd help out around the compound—hauling water from the river, planting and watering the crops we hoped could help feed us, shoring up defenses where they were needed.

Afternoons I usually spent talking with Milton. He never tired of it. I smiled that it had taken the zombie apocalypse for a scientist and an English professor to appreciate and discuss the finer, more humane points of civilization. On balance, perhaps it was not the most surprising irony one could imagine, but it was still funny.

Some evenings I spent with Tanya, far too few for my taste. She was devoted to Popcorn and spent most of her time with him, reading with him, helping him with his mathematics lessons. It was nice to see them together, as they both obviously needed it very much.

On the other hand, I was constantly reminded of how much I disliked other people's children, and the fact that this one was

the most extreme charity case imaginable only slightly offset that. I was honest enough to admit—only to myself, of course, never to Tanya—how much I resented him for threatening or diminishing what little opportunities I had to work on a sexual or romantic relationship with her. But a couple evenings with Tanya were better than I had expected ever to have again, and much better than I deserved.

On balance, like Milton's meager little Christmas among the undead, everything was a lot better than I had dared hope for, under the circumstances, and it made me quite optimistic for the future.

I learned that, spats and posturing notwithstanding, Jack did have an infrequent and more or less completely physical relationship with Sarah. I usually smiled at it, seeing how right Milton was that categorizing people made it so much easier to understand them and work around their idiosyncrasies. Whereas some objective standard of morality might have made the relationship of Jack and Sarah seem wrong, seeing it from Jack's rational point of view made it much easier to appreciate and weigh its merits.

As Jack explained it—in completely rational, cost-benefit terms—the physical relationship was satisfying to both, and the relationship brought Sarah some increased status among the women in the community, by attaching her to the strongest male leader and removing the stigma of not having a mate or children. Though Jack didn't include it in his list of benefits, I could've added that it also removed him from the inconveniences of sexual advances from either males or females in the group, thereby cutting down on jealousy and competition, as well as eliminating any doubts about his potency or preference, making it easier for him to command.

But, of course, to understand a relationship was not the same as to want to imitate it: I wanted something more with Tanya, but was also willing to wait until the opportune time.

Further complicating this was the initiation rite. I learned that Tanya and Popcorn would be the next ones going out. Milton explained they could've added an age requirement to exclude Popcorn until later, but it hardly made sense in his case. If anything, they were afraid he'd grow more sullen and withdrawn if he didn't have this to work for. It made sense for me to go with them, though there was precedence in the community for two people to go out with someone who had already been initiated as a full citizen, if a suitable, new, third person was not ready at the time of their initiation. But I told Jack and Milton that I would be going with them, and everyone seemed happy with that.

The day before our big outing, I was sitting up with Tanya, back in the recreated frontier cabin. Jack had been kind enough to sneak us a bottle of wine on his last raid to the supermarket, and Tanya was considerate enough to me that she tucked Popcorn in early. But the evening was still mostly business. Using various utensils and crockery, Tanya was recreating a map of the city on the table and going over the plans for tomorrow.

"If we head west, we can see what's in this part of the town. The hospital's there." She set a cup down on the table to represent the hospital. "The only other things I remember there were offices and some restaurants, so we might not find anything. By that time, it should be getting sunny and hot, so we should be alone on the streets. Then if we turn south, there's a big grassy hill, with the library in the middle of it. Depending on how far south we go, we can make it across the bridge right in front of the museum, or across the next one down. If we do that, we'll be in the park, but it's just a few hundred yards before we're back here and we're done."

I looked at her. I'd thought she was stunning from the first, but candlelight and familiarity and respect only compounded it; I hadn't been so smitten since I met my wife back in college. "You know, whatever happens, I think it'd be nice if the kid made it back." It wasn't quite what I'd expected to say, but I'd turned into such a lightweight when it came to drinking that it didn't surprise me when I blurted out things I might have rethought, if given the chance. Living on a diet of mostly burnt biscuits and canned peaches, I guess it made sense that a half bottle of wine would go to my head and drop my guard this way.

Tanya's eyes sparkled and she smiled. "Jonah, coming on to me by acting like you're interested in Popcorn when I know damn well you're not? Oh my, you are slick. Jack would just say something crude and flex his biceps, the big, macho doofus."

I put my hand on hers and said, "I love you, Tanya." I really hadn't been planning on that, either.

She raised an eyebrow and leaned close. She was trying to hide it, but she was as tipsy as I was. We weren't the first couple to ease the awkwardness with alcohol. "I think I knew that, Jonah, but thanks for saying it. Most men take way too long getting around to the saying part. And I don't think now's the time to be taking too long saying things."

She put her other hand on mine. Then she leaned across the table, and we kissed, just lightly at first. Between kisses, she breathed, "I love you, too." Then she leaned back. "You're not going to ruin everything by saying, 'Let's make love,' are you?" She smiled as she asked it.

I'm sure I had the usual crushed look that men always have in that situation. "Why not?"

She walked around the table, and I stood up. She started kissing my neck, working up to my ear. "Because it sounds goofy as hell when a man says it." She leaned back and put her forefinger on my lips. "But don't say it the other way, either. Just don't talk." Then she really kissed me.

I'd never been a prizefighter, and I'd never stormed the beach on D-Day or gone over the top of the trench at the Battle of Verdun. But if I remembered the film conventions appropriate to each type of combat, then I knew it was imperative—indeed, a matter of life and death—that one never have sex before the big fight. Yet it was equally imperative to lose one's virginity before going into battle in the war to end all wars. As I kissed Tanya more and more passionately, as my hands found her breasts and then her buttocks, I decided that, even though I wasn't a virgin, what *was* the war to end all wars if not the one we were in?

That night, I found that Tanya's passionate nature extended to something other than fighting and raising kids. And between her extremely muscular thighs, on some musty, 150-year-old quilt, I got much, much more optimistic about the future.

Chapter Nine

We were up before dawn, on the museum's roof with Jack, Milton, Popcorn, and some others. Popcorn, Tanya, and I were all wearing denim jackets and jeans for the little protection they'd afford us from bites. In the summer heat, though, it would wear us down quicker, so we each had to carry a canteen to offset dehydration.

Jack handed each of us a walkie-talkie. "The bridge to the north is pretty clear, so we'll send a vehicle across if you call. They should be able to pick you up pretty quick wherever you are. We'll watch all the bridges. When we see you coming across, we'll distract the stiffs away from either the front or the back gate to let you in."

On a table, Jack had set the weapons he had chosen for us. To Popcorn he gave four spikes—huge nails about ten inches long. I remembered having aluminum ones almost that long for sticking in baked potatoes, but these were thicker and looked a little rusty, although the couple inches closest to the point were all silvery, like someone had been sharpening them.

"Remember what we went over," Jack said. "Stab them in the eyes, ears, or temples. And no throwing!"

To Tanya he gave the particularly brutal weapon of a machete. "Careful with that thing: I've been sharpening it every night."

"Oh, Jack, now I know you care," Tanya teased. "Or did Sarah finally come to her senses, and you've been lonely at night, playing with your big, sharp 'machete'?"

Jack cocked an eyebrow at her, but he was smiling, too. "Easy, gal, the stiffs aren't known for their sense of humor, and we need yours back here."

He handed me an aluminum baseball bat and smiled. "I think this has always been your weapon. Be careful."

He took us over to his favorite little addition to the museum, his insane zip line across the river. The sun was just coming up behind us, and I could begin to make out the gloomy streets and buildings of the dead city. Looking down the zip line, I had a clear view of where I'd touch down, and one man was watching the landing zone through the scope of a rifle. Never mind the dead on the other side; the main fear I had was how long the zip line was: it must've been well over five hundred feet across the museum grounds, the river, and into the city. "Jack," I said, "how fast are we going to hit the other side?"

"Not a problem. The slope is really shallow. Some people have actually gotten stuck in the middle, but if that happens, you can just drop in the river, and we can pick you right up. If you're to the other side, you'd be close enough to the ground that you should be able to drop off. But with you three, I'd only worry about Popcorn not having enough momentum, since he's so small, so he should go second. Tanya could knock him along if she had to, and hopefully not lose all her momentum."

Jack handed us each a leather belt. "They're all greased up

in the middle, so don't touch them there. Put it over the cable, wrap the ends around your wrists, and give yourself a good push off the edge here. All of you be careful."

"Good luck," said Milton. "Don't take any unnecessary risks, and hurry back to us."

Part of me still thought the whole thing was an unnecessary risk, but I wanted to prove myself to the group. I'd lived for weeks on my own out there; a few hours with two people who were fairly brutal and efficient killers should be easy. I was pretty confident neither of them would get careless, and I knew I wouldn't.

I got up on the edge of the roof and did as Jack instructed. I'd never been afraid of heights, but this was definitely daunting, looking down the four stories to the ground, then scanning the hundreds of feet across the river. There was nothing to do about it but just go. I launched myself forward and started sliding along the cable. As Jack had said, it was a fairly slow and steady ride. I let go as my feet were about to hit the ground, then rolled forward and got up without too much difficulty.

Popcorn was right behind me. I caught his legs as he came sliding across the cable, so I could stop his descent before he let go. I did the same for Tanya. Then all three of us started forward, down the middle of the street to avoid anything hiding in doorways.

As Tanya had planned, we would move straight ahead, up a slight hill to the hospital. The stores and restaurants in this part of town were all thoroughly ransacked, and we saw no sign of the dead as we worked our way west among the abandoned cars.

When we got to the third large cross street, we saw the

hospital on the northwest corner of the intersection, definitely a scene of much greater carnage and destruction than mere looting and ransacking. Most of the hospital's windows were smashed out, and from some, the blinds were flopping in the wind. Above others, blackened marks reached up the side of the building, as though many rooms had been on fire, with the flames licking upward. Since the building was still standing, most of this must've happened in the first few days of the crisis, when there was still water-pressure in the sprinkler system to put out the fires.

The wrecked cars in front of the building were especially dense, essentially shutting off the entrance, and many of them were also badly burned, as though they had kept coming there and crashing, even when the wrecks were already two deep and up on the sidewalk. I couldn't help but shake my head at the sign above the entrance: "MERCY HOSPITAL."

I had thought perhaps of checking out the building when Tanya had mentioned it the night before, but it didn't look too inviting now. With such a traffic jam in front of the doors, I couldn't even see any way in. "Come on," she whispered, "let's go. I hated hospitals before this, and now they must be crawling with them. Let's go."

Just then we heard a wail. At a smashed-out window on the third floor, one of the dead had spotted us. It wore a nurse's uniform, covered in blood, and was partly burned all over. It was pointing at us.

The room behind her must've been crowded with other zombies, for at her signal of new prey, they pressed forward and toppled her out the window. She flipped in the air and landed on her back with a horrible, dull thud. The impact was hard enough that her upper torso and arms bounced up, then flopped back down. The fall must've broken her back, as her arms kept writhing and her head kept lolling around, yet she made no move to get up.

As my gaze moved back to the window, another zombie crawled onto the sill. It was burned so badly I couldn't tell what it had been in life. The others pushed it out. Unlike the other, it landed face first, a more fatal landing, as the head snapped back, then flopped forward, and the whole body stayed still. Mercy Hospital was continuing to claim victims.

More zombies stood at the window, flailing and clamoring and killing themselves to get at us. I turned to see both Tanya and Popcorn just as mesmerized by the grotesque display of undead, human lemmings. And I saw, almost at the same time as I smelled its hideous stench, a zombie's rotted hand reaching for the back of Tanya's neck.

As I shoved her to the side, I raised the baseball bat up with my left hand.

The zombie wore coveralls. He was hunched over, his right arm out in front, his head lolled to the left. The right side of his face had been torn off, revealing blackened teeth through flayed flesh and caked blood. The right eye had been gouged out as well, leaving a black, sightless hole. And as I pushed Tanya out of the way, I could see he still clutched a hammer.

Though it happened frequently—either when zombies obsessively clutched things they had been holding when they died, or when their random groping latched onto something—there was still an extra element of terror in seeing a zombie wielding a weapon. It wasn't that it made the creature more dangerous: their insatiable, plague-contaminated teeth would always be their most terrifying weapon.

No, seeing them clutch anything made by human artifice—a hammer, a pistol, or, in one of my most horrible visions, a little girl's doll—was a terrible reminder of what we all tried desperately to overlook every minute of the day: that the undead were not some alien invader that had descended upon us. They were what we, the temporarily living, would inevitably become, each and every one of us—a rotting, tottering, mindless parody of ourselves.

I gave a backhanded blow with the bat. It smashed him across the mouth, sending teeth flying like a shower of bloody raisins, snapping his head around, and making him stagger back. I grabbed the bat again with both hands and raised it high to finish him, but he raised his one good eye to look at me. As usual, there was no emotion or feeling in his eye—not rage, not fear—but, like the hammer in his hand, they held just enough residual humanity to make him both horrible and pitiable.

He reared up, growling, wheezing, and raising both his arms. Whether it was to attack with the hammer or to ward of my blow, it was completely impossible to tell.

With a sudden flash to my right, Tanya's machete went through his left wrist and neck. The hammer, with the bloodless hand still clutching it, clanked at my feet, while his head fell to the left and rolled under a car. The remaining limbs and trunk stayed where they were, the right leg and arm twitching slightly.

Tanya took a step forward and shoved it to the ground. "Son of a bitch! Try to touch me, you son of a bitch!" She wiped the machete blade on the leg of his coveralls, then stood up and spat on him. I remembered my little ritual over the dead, and knew she would think I was either stupid or crazy for doing it, just as I was feeling increasingly uncomfortable with her savagery. But I also knew there was no sense judging her. As bestial as our lives had become, the only question was how to maintain some respect and humanity among the living: whether you did it by granting some tiny shred of respect to the dead, or by completely dishonoring them, that was a choice you had to make for yourself, based just on what drove you the least crazy.

I looked around. Fortunately, Headless had not brought any of his undead friends along.

I looked Tanya over. She was panting, teeth gritted, veins bulging out of her neck, sweat on her brow, and she was holding the blood-smeared machete down with her left hand. Like Milton said, such an unbelievable and frightening amount of rage. I'd never seen a lover decapitate someone trying to kill us; it was as disconcerting as I would've imagined, though strangely arousing in some savage, primal way. I guess you'd know she'd always have your back, and if anyone could raise and defend your kids in this insane, charnel-house of a world, it had to be her. But you really didn't want to piss her off.

I grabbed her by the arm, and we all ran toward the grassy plaza across the street, trying to escape for just a minute the endless violence of both the living and the dead.

The large grassy hill of the plaza occupied six city blocks: three north-south by two east-west. On the corner near where we entered, we saw a playground, with trees, fountains, statues, and benches throughout the park. The dead seemed to have deserted the place in the heat of the late morning sun. As we ran along one of the walkways, the wails from the hospital receded, though I swore I could hear a different, higher-pitched sound from somewhere else nearby. It faded as well as we ran.

We stopped under a tree to catch our breath and saw no dead in pursuit from the hospital, so we calmed down a little. At the westernmost edge of the plaza, at the top of the hill, there was a large, modern building of glass and concrete, four stories high. Popcorn pointed to it. "We going to the library?"

Tanya looked at me. "You want to? I don't see any of them. It looks pretty good, and we can see all around if any start coming from the buildings at the edge of the square."

"Yeah, I think we should. You know how Milton loves books." I looked at Popcorn and smiled, though I knew pleasantries or kidding around were wasted on him. "Besides, you probably need some more books to help kids with their lessons, don't you?"

Popcorn glared at me. "Don't make fun of me, old man, just 'cause you're sleeping with her." I knew I could always count on him to remind me why I didn't like other people's children, tragedies notwithstanding.

Tanya had said they avoided pissing Popcorn off, but like I just said, you really didn't want to piss her off, either. She grabbed him by the ear and yanked him around. "'Her'? Who's she—the cat's mother?" she hissed. "Now, I know you didn't just call me 'her.' And I know you didn't say anything disrespectful."

The kid flushed and squirmed. Even in our mad world, I was glad there were people like Tanya, not just to chop off zombies' heads, but more importantly, to make sure that human relations stayed on the right footing. "No, Ms. Wright."

She yanked his ear so he was facing me. "Now, say you're sorry to Mr. Caine, too."

He glared at me twice as sourly as he had before, with his eyes narrowed to slits and his teeth bared, but his back was to Tanya. "I'm sorry, Mr. Caine."

"Thank you, Popcorn, but I'm not sure this is the time. Let's get going."

We made it up the hill to the library, still with no sign of the dead. All the windows on the ground floor were smashed out, but on the upper floors, almost all were intact. There were no signs of a fire or other damage. With so many windows, and with nothing of immediate, practical value inside, I doubted anyone had tried to hole up in there, so it hadn't been the site of a siege or a pitched battle.

We stepped through the broken glass doors and into the main reference room. It had been cursorily ransacked, with most of the books and magazines still there, just scattered around on the floor, but with the windows gone, everything had been ruined by the weather. With the whole east side of the building being windows, the room was well lit. We still seemed to be alone. "Let's go upstairs," I said.

"You sure?" Tanya never sounded nervous, but she definitely sounded like she didn't like or approve of the idea.

I kept looking around. "There's nothing worth taking here. There aren't any of them on this floor, so they probably aren't upstairs. And if there are, we can always just run out here. And we can still see if any are coming from other buildings, like you said."

I should've remembered Milton's analysis: I was giving logical arguments, and that would've worked with Jack, but I could see that Tanya just had a bad vibe from the place. On

the other hand, I also suspected there weren't many buildings outside the museum where you wouldn't get a bad vibe. Most of all, I knew I had to have books—I *had* to—and Milton had observed the power that my will had over me.

I led the way to the back of the reference room, to the stairwell door. It was a fire door and had a small window, the kind made out of glass with wire mesh embedded in it. The stairwell beyond was pretty dark, but I couldn't see any immediate threats. I motioned to Tanya to get ahead of Popcorn and be ready. I opened the door.

The light from the room made it much easier to see in the stairwell, which still looked empty. There were no sounds of anything moving on the stairs, either. I went in, and we started going up as quietly as possible.

We made it to the second floor landing, and I looked through the window on the fire door there, into a big room of books. It looked relatively undisturbed, with still no sign of the dead anywhere. We entered. At the southern end of the room, to our right, another fire door gave access to a second set of stairs. Some bookshelves lined the walls, and a row of them ran down the one side of the room.

On the other side, by the windows, there were tables, study carrels, chairs, and the dried-up remains of several large potted plants. Only one window was broken, and the plant by the broken window had gotten enough rain to survive and was looking quite hale, while its fellows were just dried sticks. Funny how the same rules apply in any kingdom—plant, animal, or undead. Sometimes you're in the right place at the right time and you survive, while the guy next to you is killed and eaten. And sometimes the guy next to you does fine, and you're dinner. Funny.

Although some of the furniture was tossed about, again there didn't seem to be any signs of a battle or siege—no blood, bullet holes, bodies, or burn marks. With only one broken window, there was no weather damage to the books. I thought of giving Milton directions, so he could come here whenever he liked, since it was a lot less risky for him. I walked over to the row of book shelves, while Popcorn climbed onto a desk by the door and Tanya looked at the shelves along the wall.

On this floor, we were in the fiction and poetry section, which was just what I wanted, of course, either for myself or Milton. We had brought a duffle bag for our finds, and I laid it on the floor, unzipped it, and started tossing books into it. I wanted them all, but books were about the heaviest thing we could choose to bring back. On the other hand, we had to hurry, so I couldn't pore over every choice. My earlier kidding aside, I also knew that Tanya really did like to teach Popcorn and the other kids, so I asked her to pick some as well, while I walked over to the windows.

I looked down on the plaza, and saw no motion whatsoever. It was a hot and sunny day, so maybe we would get lucky and all the dead would stay indoors. From this position on the second floor, plus the elevation of the hill, I could see the roof of the hospital—and the EMS helicopter parked there. I would have to tell Jack about that, though I doubted we could get to it.

Looking back down at the floor of the library, I was again surprised, this time by a woman's purse on the floor by one of the carrels. I gave it a nudge with my foot, and some stuff spilled out—a wallet, Kleenex, lipstick, a bottle of Tylenol, and a bottle of nail polish. Pink with sparkles, to be exact. I grinned as I picked up the Tylenol and the nail polish. I walked over to Tanya, tossed the Tylenol into the bag, and handed her the other little bottle. She wrinkled her nose at me. "I don't think I've worn nail polish since before I was married, Jonah."

"Milton asked for it."

She cocked an eyebrow at me. "Are you saying that . . . you know . . . that he's . . ." She shot a glance over to Popcorn and lowered her voice. "You mean that he plays for the other team? Not that there's anything wrong with that . . ."

I smiled. "No, I didn't mean it was *for* him, I just meant he asked *for* it. I mean, he mentioned it. I mean . . . just slip it in your pocket. Books ready to go?"

"Sure," she said as she zipped up the bag.

I tested the duffle to see how much it weighed. It was heavy, but not impossible to carry. We could even pick up something else small, if we saw anything on the way back to the museum.

As I turned toward the door we had come in, I heard Popcorn hiss, and saw him crouching on top of the desk he had been sitting on.

The handle on the door next to him was moving.

Like the zombies on the third floor of the hospital, the ones in the stairwell must've been pushing on the one at the front of their group, because the door suddenly opened and the first zombie staggered in, almost falling on its face.

Before Tanya and I could run to help Popcorn, he'd launched himself off the desk, just as he'd leapt the first time I watched him train. He hit the zombie from the side, driving a spike through its right temple as he brought the other spike

down on top of its head. He spun in midair, twisting the spikes and pulling them free.

As Popcorn landed on his feet, the zombie—what had been a middle aged woman, still wearing her glasses—swayed for a moment, eyes rolling back in her head, tongue lolling. Then she slumped to the side.

Tanya and I rushed over to Popcorn as the second zombie made it through the door. Pushed by its fellows, it tripped over the first zombie and fell on its face. I brought the bat down, smashing its skull and spattering its rotten, reeking brains on the front of my jacket.

Popcorn, meanwhile, had thrown himself at the door and was trying to force it shut, but one undead hand was clutching the edge of the door and stopping him from closing it. I got next to him, and we pushed as hard as we could. With a popping and crunching sound, the door severed the four dried-up fingers and closed all the way. The fingers fell to the floor in a pile of desiccated flesh that I knew I'd remember the next time we ate Vienna sausages back at the museum.

As Popcorn and I struggled to hold the door shut, Tanya slid the biggest table over and told us to get out of the way. Popcorn went first, and then I slid aside just as they slammed the table against the door. Eventually, the zombies could push past this barricade, but we only needed time to get to the other stairwell.

Unfortunately, as I looked on in surprise and alarm, the other fire door opened, and in lurched another big, fat, lethal pile of undead flesh.

Chapter Ten

I DIDN'T KNOW where the hell they were all coming from, but it was definitely becoming a problem. It was as if every floor *except* the first was crawling with the book-loving undead. I raced to the other side of the room, and with a snarl, I shoved the end of the bat into the forehead of the first zombie. It had been a large man, and it staggered into the ones behind it.

Still wielding the bat more like a spear, I hit the zombie in the forehead again. I shoved it all the way back into the stairwell, throwing the other zombies off balance. I shut the door, then threw myself against it. Immediately, the undead began to beat on it.

"Popcorn, leave Tanya to hold that table, and slide one over to me!"

Popcorn sprang to do so, and we secured the door. But now, if we stepped away from the tables on either side of the room, the dead would start to push past our barricades. Plus, both entrances were now blocked, and we had no idea how many were in the two stairwells. I was struggling to make a plan, and half considering just calling on the walkie-talkie to finish it. "The window!" Tanya said.

"Yeah," I agreed. "Go look out the window, Popcorn, make sure the lawn isn't crawling with them!"

He ran to the window. "No," he answered, shaking his head, "nothing out there. It's still deserted."

"Good," I said. "What's under the windows? Concrete? Grass?"

He leaned a little out the broken window. "Bushes. It doesn't look too bad."

"Okay. Toss the bag of books out, then go out the window. Tanya, go out right after him, then I'll go."

She nodded. It wasn't much of a plan, but it would have to do. The windows went from the floor to the ceiling in this room, so it was just a matter of stepping through the broken one and hoping the bushes broke our fall.

Popcorn dragged the bag across the floor and heaved it out the window. He watched it land, then jumped right after it. As soon as he had gone out the window, Tanya was across the room and had stepped through the opening after him. I heard the bushes rustle both times, and no screams, so those were good signs. But the door Tanya had been securing immediately started to open; undead hands wriggled around the edge, their eager, greedy fingers grasping. I could hear their moaning now, rising in pitch, almost as though they sensed victory, and it even seemed as if the zombies pushing against my door redoubled their efforts in response.

I left my table and ran to the window. Better to get out before they could see where I went, so they might not dive out the window after us. If the fall didn't kill us, it definitely wouldn't hurt the undead, and we'd have a mob of them chasing us down the lawn, plus however many their moaning attracted.

Outside, Tanya and Popcorn waited for me several yards

away. I took the step out the window. The bushes were a good break for the fall.

The three of us ran down the hill, heading for some trees near the southeast corner of the plaza. I kept looking over my shoulder to see if any of the dead were tumbling out the window after us, but none were.

At the trees, we stopped and looked around. We were all pretty hot and worn out, so we drank from our canteens and tried to calm down a little. No question that it had been tense in the library, but now we were out and halfway done with our work. We moved quietly along the street, heading east toward the river.

As Tanya had said, most all the storefronts were restaurants or office buildings, useless to explore, but one undisturbed window caught all our eyes. It was a toy store, of all things. The window wasn't smashed, and everything looked as though it hadn't been disturbed in a year. Like most non-chain toy stores, it was extremely high-end stuff—Brio, Playmobil, Steiff—all stuff that I'd never been able to afford. I tried the door, but it was locked.

"Too bad," I whispered. "Jack seemed excited about people raising kids."

"Forget it!" Tanya whispered.

"Yeah, I guess so." Just then, a human form emerged from the gloom in the store. He had been an older man. There were no big wounds on him, but his right forearm, mouth, and chin were covered with dried blood. He must've crawled in there to die, locked himself in, and been trapped since.

Something about us really set him off. Maybe it had been his store, and some part of him still regarded us as vandals and thieves. With a gurgling roar, he raised his two bony fists above

his head and charged at the door. His head and fists all hit the glass at the same time, and it was enough to smash through. And all that glass shattering and crashing to the ground was loud—really loud.

Loud enough to wake the dead, you might say.

The zombie storekeeper staggered onto the sidewalk with us. Tanya dropped the bag so she could wield the machete better. But she didn't need to. Popcorn was behind the guy, and that's the only opening we needed. The boy sprang onto his back and plunged both spikes into the old guy's temples.

The zombie's hands flew up, his eyes rolled back, and he took one step forward before falling on his face. As soon as he did, Popcorn was back on his feet, but he was pointing into the store and gasping, "Look out!"

An old lady zombie was coming at us through the shattered door. She was hunched over almost double. The left shoulder of her dress was shredded and soaked in blood from two massive wounds on her neck and shoulder. I guessed she had been the old guy's wife. He must've eaten her after he turned, and they'd gotten to spend nearly a year getting cozy in the store together. In a different situation, I would've found their story touching and sad, but right now all I could think was that "Till death do us part" made a lot more sense.

She was nearly on Popcorn, so I swung the baseball bat upward into her face. The blow straightened her up to a standing position, and she staggered back a couple steps into the store. I went in after her and brought the bat down hard. It crushed her skull, splattering her brains onto the wall next to her.

As she fell backward, I turned to go, but I knew that I had to have something for all this trouble. These two territorial bastards had just alerted half the town; we'd be lucky to get out alive now. I grabbed a stack of Playmobil sets with my free hand and stepped out the door.

"What are you, nuts?!" Tanya yelled as I tossed them into the duffle bag and shouldered it. All over, the dead were coming out of doors. Fortunately, there seemed to be a lot more of them back toward the plaza, while the way to the river still looked passable.

"Out in the street! Between the cars!" I yelled. "Popcorn, get up on the cars, you can move faster! Go! Go!"

Tanya was ahead of me, with Popcorn jumping from car to car next to us. The dead were mostly staggering around on the sidewalks, bumping into each other and into the wrecked vehicles, so it wasn't as bad as it had seemed.

"Up ahead, on the right!" Popcorn warned us. A big, dead guy had navigated between the cars and was moving to intercept us. Tanya didn't hesitate. The machete flashed, and the headless trunk swayed a second before collapsing to the pavement.

I heard Popcorn give a yelp. A zombie from the sidewalk had grabbed his left ankle and had tripped him up. Tanya shrieked and ran back toward us as I jumped onto the car bumper.

The zombie was pulling Popcorn by the ankle as it pulled itself onto the car hood to sink its teeth into his leg. I couldn't get a good swing at its head; Popcorn was in the way.

He wriggled around and, shoving the zombie's face back with his foot, he plunged a spike into its left ear. Popcorn twisted the spike around in its brain before pulling it out.

The zombie's head snapped back, its eyes wide, like it had just heard something really interesting. Then it twitched, lost its grip, rolled onto its left side, and slid off the hood, leaving a long trail of thick, black blood across the metal. Popcorn rolled over and got up.

"Get between us!" I said to him as he jumped off the car.

We reached the street that ran beside the river and looked back. The zombies were bouncing around between the cars like marbles in an old pachinko game, working their way toward us, but they were seriously slowed down. We could still make it.

The bridge that led directly to the museum entrance was to our left, but there were a few dozen of them coming from that direction. Considering the slothful habits of zombies, they could have been the remnants of the mob that had pursued me a few weeks before. The other bridge to our right would take us into the park, and we made for that.

When we got to the far side of the bridge, we looked back again. The mob moving parallel to the river had been joined by those zombies that had managed to navigate the maze of wrecked cars down the perpendicular street, and now the growing horde was following us to the bridge. They moved so slowly, but they never tired or got distracted, and they'd never relent, so we couldn't slow down.

The park was foreboding, with too many trees for my liking right now. We started down one of the walkways, and all I could think of was Dorothy and her friends in the *Wizard of Oz* and "Lions, and tigers, and bears! Oh my!" Unfortunately, we had much worse things to fear in there.

We worked our way along slowly and quietly, looking at every tree as though it were a threat. I kept looking back at our pursuers: they had reached the end of the bridge on the other side of the river. We were doing all right, if we could just keep moving like this—but then I heard a growl. A zombie had come out from behind a tree and was coming for us.

Tanya stepped toward it, raising the machete. She buried the blade in its forehead, all the way down to the middle of its face. She had to put her foot in its chest to pull it out.

Then something hit me in the shoulder, and Popcorn yelled, "Look out!"

I turned and stepped back to see a huge, lumbering figure right at my side. It must've been a motorcycle or equestrian cop because it wore that kind of helmet, with the visor down. Its left arm had been torn off at the shoulder, leaving a dangling mass of ragged flesh with one thick bone sticking out and a bloodstain running the length of its body. In its right hand, it still held its police baton, which is what it had hit me with.

I swung the bat and connected solidly. Its head jerked to one side, but came right back to an upright position. The helmet was enough to protect it from my blows.

Quickly, Popcorn dodged under the cop's raised arm and drove a spike up under its chin. It probably hadn't gone that far into its brain because the zombie started to twitch, and its head slumped forward, looking down at Popcorn as it raised the baton again.

Before it could strike, I shoved it backward. It toppled over and lay on the grass, writhing, perhaps unable to get up.

We started moving forward again. But then, as I looked at a big tree ahead and to the right, an indistinct, dark shadow at its base started to move and resolve into separate, distinct figures.

I pulled Tanya by the elbow to the left, but she pointed to a tree there, where a similarly sized group was rising slowly to their feet. After a few seconds, we saw another group even farther to the left, and another one directly in front of us.

As they ended their siesta and started their pursuit, they set up their low moaning, and my skin crawled. They slowly rose and walked, forming an undead wall between us and the museum. And the pursuing mob behind us was halfway across the bridge. We stopped, then started inching back.

"Uh, guys, we may have to think about getting citizenship some other day," I whispered. "As embarrassing as it might be, I think it's time we asked the cavalry to come get us."

"I don't think they'd get here in time," Tanya replied. "There are too damned many of them, and they're closing too quick. We need a place to make a stand until help gets here."

"There!" Popcorn pointed to a large clearing by the river, with a bandstand in the middle.

"All right," I agreed, "go, go!"

We ran to the bandstand and went inside. Past it, a wall dropped about six feet to the river. We'd be able to hold them for a while, even once they got to us. Like every bandstand, it had only one entrance, with a low fence around the rest of the platform. The platform itself was raised two feet off the ground, and a hedge surrounded it as well, making it harder for them to get at us quickly from anywhere except the one entrance.

"Jack?" I said into the walkie-talkie.

"We're here, Jonah. We saw you come across the bridge. Where are you?"

"On a bandstand in the park. We need help."

"That's okay. Milton went out looking for you. Just sit there one more minute."

From under the trees, the first of them came out into the light of the clearing. As in the convenience store, they were all races and ages and sizes. And they all had only one thought left in their rotted brains—to bite into our warm flesh.

About a dozen had entered the clearing when we heard the moaning trail off. Milton ran toward us, bashing several of them in the head with a large staff. He got to the step up to the bandstand. "Stay close to me!" he said. "Walk along right on the edge of the wall by the river. I'll clear a path through them. You've only got a little ways more to go."

We did as he said. He walked in front and slightly to our right, arms out, trying to keep them away. Fortunately the mob from the bridge still hadn't reached us, so we only had to make it past the ones from under the trees. They would approach, cringe from Milton, but then reach for us as the hunger overcame whatever fear it was that they had of him.

Popcorn was in the very middle of the three of us. I was in front, and if one got too close, I'd have to give it the bat across the head, or simply shove it into the river, though it was hard for me to strike or grab over Milton's outstretched left arm. Tanya was bringing up the rear, and more of them were getting around Milton's right arm to clutch at her. She lashed out with the machete, careful of Milton when she struck. We inched along, with Tanya leaving a trail of heads and arms along the river wall behind us.

After just a couple minutes, we were out of the park and crossing the street to the museum. The cherry pickers were raised again, and as we neared, the gates opened and people came out to help us the way they had the day I arrived. This time, there was no mob of undead; we easily entered, and the gates were secured behind us.

Milton embraced all of us, bloody and reeking though we were. He raised our hands with his, and the crowd gave us a cheer. At least we were home.

Milton walked into the sculpture garden and climbed onto the base of one sculpture. "Friends, we must decide now on the status of our brave warriors, whether their partial victory is enough to grant them citizenship. I can only counsel you that many times we have decided the spirit and not the letter of the law should prevail in our community. Jack, could you please present the case and examine them?"

I hadn't heard about this part of it. Maybe there was no set protocol for deciding disputable cases and Milton was just making it up. It would be like him. I knew that he liked the theatrics of the whole thing, and I couldn't blame him for his showmanship.

Jack came forward and stood under Milton. "Citizens, these three have gone out, fought, and brought back prizes for the community. They did all this with one of their group, as brave as he is, being only a boy. Within sight of our gates, Milton went out to help them—before they could ask for our help. However, they did, in fact, radio me for help before Milton found them. This is the evidence before you today."

Milton called for questions from the group. "How many did they kill?" someone asked.

I paused to count: the one by the hospital, two in the library, two at the toy store, two running down the street, one in the park. But it was hard to calculate. I wasn't sure I'd killed the one on the stairway in the library. And did the two who fell out the hospital window count? And did it count if we only incapacitated them, as I had the motorcycle cop? And I had no idea how many Tanya had killed as we followed Milton. I assumed I should give us the benefit of the doubt, but I was still faltering and trying to think of what to say.

"More than twenty," Tanya said loudly. For a little more effect, she raised her bloody machete and added, "Their rotten heads lie scattered all over the city!" There was a loud rumble of approval. It wasn't an impossible estimate, surely. (She told me later that it would put us over the number killed by any other group, and that she had long suspected that other groups exaggerated, too. I could see that the new community was only slightly less prone to the excesses and deficiencies of the old world.)

"And what did they bring?" someone else asked. A little greed and bribery were worked into the system too, I saw.

Jack unzipped the duffle bag. He could see the contents before the crowd did, and I could see he was considering which item to present first; to create the best effect for us, I assumed.

He held up the Tylenol. There was only a very slight rumble of approval that dissolved into whispers of, "Could come in handy . . . We don't have much left."

He held up the books, handfuls of three or four at a time. I think he showed some more than once. The approval was less than for the Tylenol.

Finally, he held up the Playmobil sets. There was a very loud, "Awww! We don't have any of those!" Okay, so they were greedy, but for their kids. As human nature went, it wasn't too bad.

After that, I was pretty sure we'd win on a decision, and we did. There was another cheer, and the crowd dispersed.

Popcorn took the Playmobil sets and went off to present them to the other kids. Tanya and I stood with Jack and Milton.

"Thanks," I said. "I hope that doesn't compromise the justice here too much."

Jack was his usual jovial self. "What? You feel bad about it? The kids got some stuff for a change. Milton got his books. And I have a feeling Tanya didn't exaggerate the body count too much, hmm?" He looked sideways at her. "People used to inflate body counts when it was real people they were killing, so they could get the budget increase they wanted. No, I don't think we're doing too badly, by human standards."

"And those are the ones we must live by, Jonah," Milton said. "We will be judged—if, God willing, there are ever again historians to judge us—by how we fared compared to other human societies. Don't be so hard on yourself.".

"You all worry about the details," Jack said as he got up to leave. "I have to check the back gate, see how they're doing with the stiffs piling up back there."

"Besides, we didn't even show them everything we got," Tanya added after Jack left. She got out the bottle of nail polish and showed it to Milton. "I'm not sure why, but Jonah said you wanted this."

Milton actually blushed. "No, no, my dear, I'm sure you misunderstood him. I think Jonah meant that he thought you might like it. It's so hard to find and present a gift to someone in our wretched world, isn't it?"

"Yes, I suppose it is," Tanya said, still eyeing the two of us as she slipped the bottle back into her pocket.

Later that evening, we were feted at another of our meager feasts, though someone was thoughtful enough to serve canned hams instead of the less appetizing varieties of canned meat to which we were condemned. Some wag even put together that glop of green beans and cream of mushroom soup that everyone has for Easter. My guilty conscience and nitpicking about rules notwithstanding, I felt almost as optimistic about the future as I had the night before.

Chapter Eleven

THE FIRST THING the next morning, I told Jack about the helicopter on the hospital roof. In hindsight, I guess it should have been counted as one of our accomplishments at our judgment the day before, but I just hadn't remembered it at the time. Jack listened with rapt attention and fascination to the details of the hospital, obviously hatching a plan.

"The buildings next to it aren't taller than the hospital, are they?"

I really hadn't remembered to note such details when I was looking at it from the library. "I don't think so."

"I don't think so either, from what I can remember. And the main entrance looks impassable?"

"Definitely. You'd need a bulldozer to push the wrecks out of the way, and even once you did, you'd be fighting off all the zombies trapped inside."

"And if they were lined up to take a dive off the third floor, it sounds like the whole inside of the place is pretty full of them."

"It sure seemed that way."

He paused to think. "Okay. I think we can send a vehicle over the bridge to the north, and have it circle around to get close

to the hospital. When the zombies come out of the hospital to investigate, it'll start to drive away. They'll follow it, then you, me, and Franny—the only person here who knows how to fly a helicopter—will sneak up there and fly it home." Jack smiled, obviously pleased and satisfied with his plan. "I even made sure I had a 24 volt battery on hand, so just in case we ever did find a chopper, we'd be able to jump start it."

"But how will the zombies be able to get out of the hospital to follow the vehicle? That was why they were falling out the window: the entrance was so blocked they were all jammed in there with no way to get out."

"Oh, now that's going to be a little bit of a fun part, if you like that sort of thing. Come with me."

Jack took me to the main exhibit hall. On the one side was an archway labeled "GEMS AND MINERALS." I'd seen it every day, but had never been inside; a big metal gate was closed across it and locked. It seemed to be part of the original design of the museum because it was the one room where they kept things valuable enough to warrant such security. I hadn't even thought that the survivors used it for anything special, but today Jack unlocked it and we went in.

The room only had the one door, with no windows, so it was dark and cool inside, like a cave, even during the day. The beam from Jack's flashlight fell on various crystals and gems, which sparkled with an unearthly magnificence. On top of several of the glass cases were laid rows of firearms and ammunition.

"This is where we keep some of the bigger or more unusual weapons, the things that we don't have in the lockers for people to grab just for everyday use." He chuckled a little. "People used to have towels that were only for special

company—we have guns and bombs that are only for special company!"

His light fell on a pile of about a dozen wooden crates, each about four feet long and ten inches square at the ends. "We brought these with us when we tried to defend the bridge, but we never got a chance to use them. I've been wondering when they might come in handy."

We stepped close enough to be able to read the lettering stenciled on them. Jack shined the light on one, and it said "M136 AT4 HEAT." He moved the light to another box that was labeled "M136 AT4 HEDP."

"What are they?" I asked, being almost completely unfamiliar with any weaponry beyond civilian handguns.

"Shoulder fired, light anti-tank weapons. If you saw it, you'd probably call it a bazooka. These are much more modern, one-shot weapons. They fire a rocket with a shaped charge, very effective against tanks and other vehicles."

"So why don't you fire them into a crowd of zombies, to blow them up?"

He smiled at my naiveté. "You got to pay attention, professor: I said they were effective—*against tanks*. The projectile carries a shaped charge, for penetrating armor, so it doesn't make a big explosion outward, or send out lots of shrapnel. That's what you'd need to take down a group of stiffs. No, these are pretty useless against the undead, I'm afraid, so here they've sat."

"They'd only be of use against other people, since only people drive vehicles."

Jack looked sideways at me, the light from the flashlight illuminating our faces from below, the way you used to hold a flashlight to scare your sister when you were little. "You know, it's a little reassuring, *and* a little sad, to meet someone as cynical

as I am. But yes, that's just what I've been thinking. If some bad guys came sniffing around here, trying to hurt us or take our stuff, these might be just the thing to make them go away."

We walked back out of the minerals gallery, and Jack locked it back up.

"Okay," I said, "so why show me now, when we're talking about getting the helicopter off the hospital roof?"

"You wanted a way to let all those zombies out of the hospital, so they could follow our vehicle away from it, and we could get in without much trouble. So why not blow a hole in the wall and let them out?"

"I thought you said it didn't make a big explosion?"

"That's why it's good we have both kinds of ammunition. It comes in two main types: 'HEAT' stands for 'high-explosive anti-tank.' That would just make a small diameter hole if we shot it at a wall. But 'HEDP' is 'high-explosive dual purpose.' They made it for taking out walls and bunkers and buildings. Still not much good against personnel, but it would make a pretty big hole in the side of the hospital. And when the dust settled, out would come the zombies. And in we'd go."

"How do you know they're all going to come marching out?"

"Oh, I don't. The blast should skrag any that are unlucky enough to be standing right by that wall. A lot of the ones who are nearby won't be able to hear for hours, so that should help us sneak in. The rest should go to investigate what's going on, like they usually do."

"What if the chopper isn't gassed up?"

"Might not be. Maybe that's why they left it up there. But even if it's down to fumes, we should be able to make it the couple of blocks to get over here."

"Sounds pretty risky. I'm not sure I'm glad I brought it up."

Jack smiled. "Hey, you risked your life for Playmobil. If this works, we're going to have a *real* helicopter on our roof. That'd make life easier, and safer."

And that was that. The plan was logical, and it had a practical, physical benefit. With Jack, once that was determined, there wasn't much discussion. So we were going the next day to try and get a helicopter.

By mid-morning, I was at the rear parking lot. We didn't leave at dawn, as we didn't expect this to take too long, and we wanted to take advantage of the relative scarcity of zombies in the midday sun.

Jack was inspecting the vehicle and its crew. It was a small dump truck, the kind a landscaping company would have. Apparently, it had been the truck assigned to help maintain the grounds of the museum and the park across the street, so it had been in the museum parking lot when the crisis began; they were lucky enough that there were keys to it in the museum. One man would drive the truck, with three in the back to fire the missile and to fight off the zombies that would try to climb up.

Jack made sure they had plenty of weapons, besides a couple of the AT4s. He was usually very conservative with ammo, as he had been the night I arrived, but to get his helicopter, Jack had armed them heavy, not just with the usual hand-to-hand weapons, but with plenty of guns and Molotov cocktails. This was to be his prize, his legacy to the community, leaving it better protected and provided for.

Once the truck crew was settled, I went with Jack to the roof of the museum. Franny was there waiting for us. She was

a tall, blonde woman with big blue eyes. She wasn't gorgeous, and just a tad butch, but with her height, blonde hair, and athletic build, she was quite striking in her own way, especially in fatigues and a flight jacket, as she was dressed now. She had been part of Jack's group and was very competent at work in general and combat in particular. If I had picked anyone for Jack to hook up with, it would've been her rather than Sarah, but I was almost always wrong about such things.

Jack reached under his jacket and pulled out my Glock and my magnum. "A man should have his own hardware," he said, smiling and handing them to me.

The plan was for the truck to go do its thing, then we'd go across on the zip line as the men in the truck led the zombies away from our goal. Jack was carrying the battery; I'm sure he was the only one of us who could, as it was heavy. We watched the truck pull out of the parking lot, the gate closing behind it. It slowly circled around, across the bridge to the north, and into the city.

In a couple minutes, they were outside the hospital. They reported over the radio that a few undead were already investigating them, attracted by the sound of the engine. Then we heard the explosion. They reported that they were driving away with a large, undead crowd in slow pursuit. "If you're going to go," the speaker said, "you should go now."

Two men looking through the scopes of rifles reported that the landing area for the zip line was clear, and we went. When we got to the hospital, there was a hole about four feet wide and five feet high in the side. Up the street, about a quarter mile away, the truck led the mob away from us. We could hear their occasional gunfire, and there was no sign of the dead in our immediate vicinity.

"The first floor should be clear," Jack whispered, "but

they're probably still all over the upper floors, so make for the stairwell and up to the roof as fast as possible. And don't make a sound."

We ran across the street and through the hole, into the hospital. As Jack predicted, the remains of several zombies lay right near the opening, either completely dead with glass and masonry stuck in their heads, or just immobilized by the flying debris shredding their legs and torsos.

We moved into the hall, which was thankfully deserted, though it was one of the more horrific building interiors I'd seen. Equipment and furniture was everywhere, with no way of telling whether it had been used as barricades, or randomly flung about by people fleeing, or shoved around by zombies in the intervening months. What seemed like millions of pieces of paper were scattered all over. Blood was everywhere, of course, some of it diluted by the sprinklers to a grimy, pink sheen, and some of it in darker splotches on the floors, or smeared across the walls in huge swatches, sometimes with handprints still visible in them. I could not imagine that the killing floor of a slaughterhouse would look any worse. But, of course, that is just what the hospital had been a few months ago.

The stairwell wasn't that far from where we came in, fortunately. As we moved toward it, a human upper torso slithered toward us in the hall. It was wearing a nurse's uniform, with bloody shreds of cloth, flesh, and intestines trailing off behind it like dried tentacles or tendrils.

I tried to step around it, while Franny brought her boot down on its head with a wet, crunching sound. Its arms, which had been reaching for Franny's foot, flew straight out, spasmed once, then went limp. Franny wiped her boot on the back of its uniform, then stepped away. Unlike Tanya, there was no anger or disgust in her movement: she would've shown more emotion stepping on a roach. I envied her, in a way.

We entered the stairwell and began to climb. It wasn't a huge hospital, only six floors, so we didn't have that far to go. The stairwell was clear, but we did duck at each landing as we passed the little windows in the fire doors, avoiding any undead eyes.

When we got to the sixth floor, we saw that the stairwell didn't go all the way to the roof. We would have to go through the building and find the one that did. Thankfully, this floor looked deserted.

However, the door had been secured. A thick chain ran from the handle inside the hall, between the door and the sill, and then was wrapped around a water pipe in the stairwell. It must've been padlocked or otherwise secured on the other side, after someone had run it around the water pipe and closed the door on it. The door couldn't close all the way, but the chain had been drawn tight enough that it couldn't be opened more than an inch, either.

Fortunately, Franny was carrying a pack with some tools that Jack thought we'd need. She got out bolt cutters, took care of the chain, and we opened the door.

The hall of the sixth floor was not nearly as ghastly as the first. People must've abandoned it sooner in the crisis, so it had not been the scene of such carnage. As we moved along the hall, we did see occasional evidence of violence, with spatters of dried blood at eye level.

When we got to the main nurses' station at the middle of the hall, boxes of baby formula, diapers, and other supplies were neatly stacked on it. We all looked at each other and shook our heads, unable to guess what had happened here.

The stairway to the roof was past the nurses' station, next to the elevators, and it didn't seem to be locked in any way. Before we went up, though, we saw a pair of double doors farther down the hall. They were chained shut and locked from our side.

The sign above the double doors said "NICU." That partly explained why this floor would be less damaged: they surely would've evacuated babies and mothers as soon as possible, thereby leaving the floor abandoned. On the doors themselves, faded red and white "BIOHAZARD" posters had been taped over the two windows, so one couldn't see inside. A crude skull and crossbones had been drawn on the door on the left. It looked like it had been done with a thick, black Sharpie. On the right hand door, "RIP" was written in big letters using the same kind of marker.

We had no reason to lift up the little posters and look inside. No reason other than curiosity, but that reason was too overpowering, even for a supremely rational person like Jack. It was yet another Pandora's box, where it was just human nature to look when you shouldn't.

As we peeled back the yellowing paper posters, I think we all wished we hadn't. We'd all seen horrible things, but I am sure none of us had seen anything like what those doors were meant to hide. That should've stayed hidden till the final trumpet blast.

The room was partially lit with a pale, jaundiced sunlight. Whoever had sealed it up had closed the blinds first, though here and there they'd been torn down. All over the room—lying, sitting, writhing, crawling over each other—was a myriad of the dead, in all the shapes and sizes the human body comes in, and with all the marks of death and decay that those bodies could bear.

Most were restrained in some way, with plastic police handcuffs binding their hands, or with straitjackets, or with bags over their heads. Some had gags on, made of belts or cloths. A few restraints had been torn off over the months, but the dead were too uncoordinated or disinterested to free themselves in their makeshift prison.

Like the nurse on the first floor, many were missing limbs or parts of their faces or torsos, with viscera and other organs spilling out. Their various open wounds had leaked every bodily fluid, and all this mortal slurry had now dried and decayed into a shiny slime all over them. They rolled around in their own insides just as cheerfully or obliviously as they would in a bubble bath, flesh reveling in flesh, with no respect or shame, and with all its hidden ugliness bursting to the surface. "Happy as pigs in shit," was all I could think.

The only thing that could be interpreted as fortunate was that the doors seemed to seal all the smell inside the room.

And like anything revolting, we could not turn away from it, as desperately as we wanted to.

"Shit," Franny whispered, "they tried to store them or contain them."

"I'll have to ask Milton what circle of hell this is," Jack whispered in disgust, pushing the corner of the poster back into place before turning away.

I'd taught Dante enough to know that this chamber of horrors resembled his description of several different circles of hell. But it was most like the last two parts of the eighth circle, where the deceitful are punished. Maybe Dante was right: we'd lied to ourselves for so long about who we are and what we want that now we'd be punished by having our faces shoved into what was basest and ugliest about ourselves—forever. "It's the eighth circle—for liars," I whispered as I turned away too.

"Really?" Jack said as we went back to the door of the stairwell up to the roof. "Remind me never to lie."

The stairwell past the nurses' station only led up to the roof, not down to the other floors, so we weren't too worried about any more nasty surprises. "Hey, grab a box of the formula," Jack said before we headed up. "We can't feed the moms enough to make much milk as it is."

I got up the stairs. The door to the roof didn't appear locked in any way. I put my hand on the handle. "Hey," Jack whispered. "Let's watch it. Get your boomstick out."

I set down the box of formula and got out the Glock. I pushed the handle. The sunlight was bright on the roof, enough to blind us for a second when the door swung open.

Framed in the light was a human figure. And it was sticking the barrel of a shotgun in my face.

Still blinded by the sun, I heard a hoarse voice pronounce, "Say something."

Even though seeing me holding a gun was probably enough to indicate I was alive, it was still a reasonable request when you saw three figures coming out of a building that had been full of the undead for months. "Ummm . . . hello? Don't shoot?" That's all I could think of.

The barrel lowered. "Wow, you're alive. How'd you get up here?" We emerged onto the roof and stood with the man with the shotgun. He was probably in his late twenties and incredibly thin, with wild brown hair and beard. "Wait—you didn't break my lock into the top floor, did you? Hey—what are you doing with my baby's formula?"

"Easy," Jack said. "We did break your lock, but we can secure it again, if you want. And we didn't know the formula was yours." He set his box down. Franny followed suit, while I had left mine on the step. "We were wondering, though, if maybe you'd want to come with us?"

"I'm not going down there, through all those things! My baby and I are fine up here!"

Though he seemed more nervous than deranged, we all looked around, fearing the guy was a little off. "Where *is* your baby?" Franny asked. I was pretty sure she was trying to get to the guy's side, flank him, in case he got too worked up and started waving the gun around again. I hoped she was planning on grabbing the gun, and not on shooting him, but I was also sure that she wouldn't hesitate. I gripped the Glock tighter.

The guy pointed to a long ladder that sloped down, bridging the gap between the hospital's roof and the roof of the building next to it. It looked pretty secure, as it had been placed over the top of a metal post on the hospital side, and it seemed to be tied down on both ends. On the other hand, you definitely would need a compelling reason to take a walk on a creaking aluminum ladder six stories up, over a crowd of hungry, walking corpses.

"In the other building," the man answered. "I come over here for formula for her."

"And you've been living like this since the outbreak? Just

the two of you?" Jack asked. I could see he was also sizing up any threat this guy might pose.

"Yes, after my wife . . . died. I didn't know what else to do, once they were everywhere and we were trapped inside our building."

"You didn't see any of our people, or make a signal?" Jack asked, still trying to figure out whether this guy was fully rational.

"I'd hear gunfire sometimes, or a vehicle's engine, but I never saw anyone. This morning I heard a huge explosion, and then when I was over here, I heard something coming up the stairs."

"Wow, that's amazing, that you made it all this time," Jack said. "But why didn't you just take all the supplies over to your building?"

"I thought it'd be good to leave some supplies in both buildings. In case they ever got into our apartment building, we could run over here and pull up the ladder. But I wouldn't want to take my baby downstairs, on that floor with that room full of those things." He shuddered and then we could see a little tent he had set up on the roof next to the helicopter. "So I set up a tent here. I know it's not much, but I didn't know how else to plan for us."

"We understand," Jack said, being both genuinely sympathetic and still trying to calm the guy down. "We know it's been hard. I'm Jack, by the way. This is Jonah and Franny."

"Frank," the guy introduced himself.

"Well, Frank, I wouldn't ask you to carry your baby through a building and a city full of those things, but Franny here can fly a helicopter. Any idea if this thing works?"

Understandably, this news did seem to brighten up Frank

considerably. "No, I don't know. I mean, I've opened it up and got inside. I put some supplies in there, too. But I don't know anything about flying one. You mean we can get out of here? Where would we go?"

"We have a safe place, just on the other side of the river," Jack answered.

"May I?" Franny asked, reaching for the helicopter's door handle, and seeming less intent on killing the guy if he acted strange.

"Oh, yes, of course," Frank stammered. "I didn't mean everything here belonged to me, it's just . . . the formula, it's for my baby . . ."

"We understand," Jack said again, as Franny got into the helicopter.

Frank had turned from enthusiasm to just wonder. "Wow, getting out of here. I had no idea. I thought we'd just stay here until everything ran out, and then . . . I didn't know what'd happen then. I didn't have any plan. I didn't want to think about it."

"Eighth of a tank of fuel, everything looks fine," Franny said as she climbed out of the chopper. "The battery's dead, of course, but we expected that."

Jack put down his backpack containing the battery and jumper cables next to the chopper. "Frank, can you go over and get your baby? Franny can help you while I get the battery hooked up."

"I've never carried her across the ladder," Frank said, setting his shotgun down on the roof and looking worried.

Jack thought a minute. "There's rope in the pack of tools, right?"

"Sure," Franny replied.

"You got a baby carrier or car seat, something you can strap her into?" he asked Frank.

"Yeah. We bought all that before she was born."

"Okay, then carry her across in that. Run the rope through the handle or strap of it, while Franny and I stand on the two buildings and hold the two ends of the rope."

It still sounded terrifying to me, but it would have to do. Fortunately, crossing the ladder only took three long strides to the other side. Frank and Franny went over to the other building, while Jack and I loaded the formula and gear into the chopper and hooked up the battery we had brought. The helicopter was big enough inside that we even went back for two more trips, to get the supplies Frank had piled up at the nurses' station.

On the second trip, we heard the door to the stairwell at the end of the hall open, and watched as the door was pushed inward. A partially decayed, burnt face peeked through the window in the door, and we could hear the moaning from others in the stairwell.

"Get to the roof," Jack whispered as he set down the box he was carrying and picked up a mop off the floor. "I think it's time we got going."

Chapter Twelve

ONCE WE WERE in the stairwell up to the roof, Jack wedged the mop between the door and the horizontal handle, making it harder to open it from the hall. Then we went upstairs. On the roof of the other building, Frank and Franny were returning to the ladder. She was carrying two suitcases, as incongruous as it looked, and he was carrying a baby in a car seat, the kind that snaps out of the base so you can carry it by a handle. We used to have one like it, for our kids. I didn't know whether to envy him for still having his child with him, or to feel sorry for him for having to raise her in this slaughterhouse we live in now. The two of them looked like "normal" people getting ready to go on a trip with their baby. Franny scampered across the ladder with the two suitcases she was carrying and walked over to us.

"Don't say anything to him," Jack said, quiet enough so that Frank wouldn't hear. "They're in the hall downstairs. Just put the stuff in the chopper and get them in and get it started, Franny." Turning his back so Frank couldn't see, he handed me a grenade. "Wait till they're in the stairwell down there, then pull the pin, throw this down, and close the door."

Franny tossed the suitcases in the back of the chopper and went back across the ladder to Frank, carrying one end of the rope while Jack held the other. Frank threaded it through the handle of the car seat and prepared to make his run across.

Holding the door open to the stairwell, I could hear them moaning down there; the mop handle banged around on the doorsill as they tried to wrench it open. I looked down at the grenade in my hand. It was so much smaller than I had imagined grenades were, but I really didn't like the idea of holding it, let alone arming and throwing it.

I looked back to the others. Frank was across, carrying the baby. I heard a cracking sound in the stairwell, and the moaning suddenly got louder.

As Franny hustled Frank and his baby over to the helicopter, he could finally see the danger we were in. "Oh, shit! You didn't say they were already in downstairs!"

"Just get in!" Jack said. "Franny, start her up! Jonah?"

The lead zombie was just coming around to the landing. In a hospital gown, horribly burned, it was using its right arm to pull itself up with the handrail; its left arm hung limp, and its legs moved stiffly.

"Okay," I said. I held the door half open with my foot and pulled the pin on the grenade.

"Frag 'em!" Jack shouted, as the helicopter's engine roared to life.

I tossed the grenade down the stairs. It bounced past the two zombies that were now up to the landing, and I quickly shut the door. The explosion wasn't as loud as I expected. Bits of shrapnel pinged off the fire door, and the dead shrieked as the jagged metal bits tore into their flesh.

I looked over at the chopper, its rotors spinning slowly.

Jack held his hand up in a "stop" gesture. "Hold the door another second!" he shouted. "Until she gets going!"

I stayed at the door, pressing against it. As the rotors picked up speed, I could hear renewed motion in the stairwell. A grenade designed to maim and kill the living wouldn't significantly deter a crowd of determined, walking dead. If anything, it would slow them down because they'd be tripping over the shattered, immobile bodies of their fallen fellows. But they would keep coming.

In a few seconds, with the rotors' noise rising to a whine, and with paper and other things blowing around on the roof, I heard fingernails scratching on the metal door—it pushed against me. I pushed back, scrambling to plant my feet, and shouted for Jack's help.

He ran over and threw his weight against the door as well. "Franny!" he shouted.

She was flipping switches and looking all over the instrument panel. "Another minute, Jack! You know I'm supposed to warm this thing up for fifteen minutes before we try to take off! And that's if it's been sitting around overnight, not almost a year!"

"It's going to have to be a little quicker today, Franny!"

Jack fumbled around under my jacket and drew my magnum. "Duck your head, Jonah!"

I hunched down, keeping my shoulder against the door. Jack pressed the barrel of the magnum against it at eye level, angled down a bit, and fired. My ears started ringing from the blast. He moved it over six inches and fired a second bullet, then moved it another six inches and fired again. I wasn't sure he hit anything, but the pressing on the door let up.

"Okay! Come on!" Franny shouted over the engine, and

Jack and I ran for the chopper. As we climbed inside, we could hear Frank's baby crying for the first time. As much as I disliked other people's kids, I couldn't blame her.

Slowly, the chopper started to lift off the roof. We were only about a foot or so high when the stairwell door swung open, and the dead staggered straight for us, seeming to find new energy at the prospect of fresh meat. Jack and I shot the two lead zombies in the face before sliding the helicopter door shut. Frank's baby redoubled its wails at the blasts from our guns.

"Franny, come on!" Jack shouted, as two zombies pressed their mangled, flayed hands up against the plexiglass.

"Just give it a minute!" she shouted back.

We were still inching upward, but now there were several zombies pressing on the side of the chopper, making it drift more and more to the side. I didn't understand the aerodynamics of it, but I had visions of us toppling off the roof, to die in a fiery explosion on the pavement.

I looked at Frank's baby. I guess calling a baby beautiful is kind of pointless: I mean, I think it's really the *idea* of a baby that's beautiful—the thing itself is usually pretty unattractive, unless it's your own. Regardless, I looked at her little crying mouth, her face so wildly pink, her eyes scrunched shut, and her little fists quivering as she held them up, and I knew the only thing I wanted in the world right then was for her to live.

I hadn't prayed during all the various horrors of the previous months, but sitting next to a baby girl on a helicopter that was tottering six stories above the street, with a growing crowd of the hungry dead banging to get in—it seemed like a good time to start. I didn't have the words, which wasn't surprising, as I'd never been much for praying before this, so I just went with the direct approach: "God, let the kid live, please." I tried to stop myself from finishing the thought with other inconvenient details, like, "Unless you haven't killed enough kids already." No sense getting off on the wrong foot when you're praying for the first time in years, and you think you're about to die a horrible death.

I looked back out the window. We were about two feet above the roof and right at its edge. The walking dead were not only moving the chopper to the side, they were causing it to spin slightly to the right. The zombie pushing right on the nose of the chopper—oblivious as ever to the dangers around him—tumbled off the edge of the roof.

In the rear, the tail rotor was swinging around toward the zombies behind us. There was a shriek and a slight jolt, and a forearm flew up through the air. A second later, a huge shower of red shot along the side of the chopper as it took the face off another one.

Franny moved the stick, spinning us the other way, and we finally started to lift faster. But then there was another, bigger jolt, and we tilted down to the left. The main rotor tore into the crowd of zombies, throwing four of them back with their heads nearly torn off. Franny fought the stick and finally righted us, getting us moving straight up and out of their reach.

"Get them off! Get them off!" she shouted. "They're throwing us off balance! The others are getting a hold of them and pulling us back down!"

I looked down and saw what had tilted us so dangerously at the end of our lift off: two zombies were hanging off the left landing skid, and the others on the roof were clutching their feet.

"Everybody grab hold of something!" Jack shouted as he slid the door back. He himself had his right arm wrapped in a

seatbelt and was reaching back to me with his left. "Grab my arm! You've got to lean out to get a shot at them!"

Suspended about twenty feet over a crowd of mindless cannibals has to be high on anyone's list of nightmares, way ahead of being in a spelling bee naked. But, if I was going to ask God to help out, I guess it was only fair to pitch in.

I grabbed Jack's forearm and he grabbed mine, then I leaned out the open door with the Glock in my left hand. I aimed at the zombie in front, which looked like it had been a doctor, with a bloodstained white coat. It was hard to aim because the zombies were rocking the helicopter and Franny was fighting with the stick. My shot hit it in the shoulder. It let go with that hand, lost its grip with the other, and tumbled back into the crowd below.

I turned to the other zombie, a young woman in a ragged dress, the left side of her face and neck chewed off. Her head lolled around, making it difficult to get a shot. I fired and hit her in the chest, but she wouldn't let go.

To hell with the head shot.

Her hands, with their death grip on the skid, were definitely not moving, so I aimed at her left wrist and fired again. Her arm ripped away from her hand, which refused to let go. And as the dozens of zombies pulled on her from the roof, her right wrist tore apart too. She fell, leaving her two hands still tenaciously gripping the skid.

The helicopter jerked to the other side as we were freed from the mob's grip, but Franny quickly righted us and pulled us up. We slowly angled off to the north, as Jack slid the door shut. We were all panting from the final crisis of taking off, and the baby was still crying uncontrollably. Frank was trying to calm her down.

"What's her name?" I asked.

"Zoey."

I almost always thought it sounded stupid when someone said that a name sounded pretty, but I couldn't help smiling and saying, "That's a really good name."

We were flying north over the city when I saw, far in the distance to the left, a thin line of smoke. I pointed it out to Jack.

"Wow, we go months without finding anyone, and now two sets of survivors in one day! Too bad we can't check it out." He leaned over Franny's shoulder. "Low on fuel, right?"

She nodded. "Very. I was just looking for the truck, and then we got to get back to the museum."

"There they are," Jack said, pointing off to the right. "They're on the bridge."

Down on the bridge that went to the north of the museum, we could see the truck. The crowd of undead from the hospital was closing on them, but was still forty or fifty yards away. I couldn't believe they hadn't moved farther while we were in the hospital, but I could see now that our ordeal had only lasted a few minutes.

Jack got them on the radio. "Guys, I don't want them following you back to the museum. See that bus in the street, with all the stiffs milling around it?"

"Sure do," came the reply.

"Put a HEAT round in it and then get the hell out of there."

"You got it."

A man stood up in the back of the truck, and a fireball

blasted out behind him. There was a huge explosion as the projectile hit a bus in the street. The gas tank of the bus exploded, and a few seconds later, so did another in a vehicle nearby. The dead were trapped among the vehicles, staggering about, wounded, burning, and collapsing to the pavement.

The truck pulled away, across the bridge and back to safety. We followed them, landing on the roof of the museum to the cheers of the community. Jack was basking in his accomplishment, and even had the unexpected prize of two new survivors, one of whom was an adorable baby. I was glad Jack didn't have to run for election, or the whole scene would have crossed over into obnoxious grandstanding.

Though the whole thing had been a complete success, I did not feel as optimistic as I had on the two previous nights. I suppose I should have, since we had saved Frank and Zoey from certain death by starvation, or worse. But there was something in the things we'd seen that tinged the whole day with a weird, diseased melancholy, a glimpse of just how bad things could get, of what was lurking right at the edge of our consciousness, of how much had to be sacrificed and stomped into a bloody mash just to give one child a chance to live on the slightly scorched outskirts of hell, rather than right in the middle of the lake of fire. If we had seen the eighth circle, it only served to remind me that we were, at best, living in the first circle, what Dante would've called "limbo," a shadowy land where those who weren't damned, but who could not be saved, spent eternity in hopelessness and sadness.

As Frank, Jack, and I sat down with a purloined bottle in the frontier cabin that night, my foreboding grew, because I suspected that hearing Frank's story of how he had survived those months would be much worse than I could imagine.

Chapter Thirteen

WE DIDN'T PUSH him. I'm sure even Jack, as optimistic and cheerful as he was by nature, could feel the dread that hung over that man. I'm sure it was why we didn't invite any others, besides the fact that we needed Sarah to baby-sit Zoey. At first, we talked about the mechanics of survival. It was always a safe topic, as everyone had some story of how they'd found food in the most unlikely ways or places, and everyone was always proud of their own resourcefulness, thrilled and amused by their own good luck.

Frank had barricaded himself in their apartment, throwing all their furniture down the stairway that led to the street. None of his neighbors were home when the attack started, so he kicked down their doors and piled their furniture on to his barricade too, till he had a jumble of wood and metal, all the way from the street entrance up to the second floor. I could imagine that it must've been quite formidable when he was done, thousands of pounds of furniture and other household items filling the stairwell. Apparently, it was the only entrance, and he felt secure that at least the undead couldn't get in.

But he could easily see that his fortress would also be a trap,

especially with a baby on board. "I was proud of what I'd accomplished, of course, to build a place that was safe for Zoey and me, but I was really worried about food and water. I put together the food supplies from all the apartments, and it was a pretty good supply, but there was nothing for Zoey. We'd had a little bit of formula on hand—they give you these goodie bags full of different stuff at the hospital when you take the birthing classes—but no one else in the building had an infant, so I had to find something for her fast."

Apparently, after the initial outbreak and complete victory of the dead, the area around the hospital had been pretty quiet, so Frank got the rather dangerous idea to cross over to the hospital roof—like all of us, he had just done what he had to; it only seemed dangerous or heroic afterwards. On the roof of his apartment building, he found some scaffolding and other equipment for cleaning windows and painting tall buildings, including the ladder that he used as a bridge between the two buildings. Like anyone would, he got excited at this point in his story, because it was the kind of plan that would've scared any of us into paralysis before all this happened, but which had saved his baby.

"I knew the sixth floor of the hospital was pediatrics," he said, "since we'd taken the tour before Zoey was born. I'd seen the things, the dead people, on television and down on the street, so I knew they were slow. All I could do was hope there weren't too many of them up on the sixth floor, and I could just grab some formula and run back to our apartment. I was just hoping to get enough for a few days, until help arrived. I got across to the hospital and didn't see or hear anything at all. The whole town smelled like hell—you remember it was summer when it happened."

"Yeah," Jack grunted in agreement, "like Satan's asshole." I couldn't help smiling at him: he probably didn't know the religious concept of the *axis mundi*—the center or navel of the world—and how some writers had inverted it to the *anus mundi* in describing places like Auschwitz. But, as usual with Jack's deep reserve of common sense, he had rightly intuited it as the aptest label for our situation.

"That's about right," Frank nodded. "But oh my God, the hospital was worse than anywhere else. You could barely stand it. So many different smells of decay and sickness and death, but with disinfectant and chemicals mixed in. You'd never have been able to imagine it before. It made you gag constantly. I was wearing a bandana over my face, to try to help with the smell, and I was carrying an aluminum baseball bat. I must've looked like some kid playing a game, dressed up like that.

"On the sixth floor of the hospital, I saw one of them there, but I ran right at it and hit it with the bat, and it went down. Another one came out of a room, and I smashed that one, too. And then it was all quiet and still again. There was a bunch of cans of formula right out where I could see them, and I grabbed those and ran. I felt so good. I'd saved Zoey. I thought now we were okay. I could just wait until help arrived."

He paused and drank before continuing.

In the days after his first trip to the hospital, Frank realized he was in this for the long haul. It was then that he wisely secured the top floor of the hospital, as we had found it, so he wouldn't have to fight zombies every time he needed supplies, and so he could retreat if his building were overrun. He had killed the few zombies on the top floor and locked the doors into the stairwells with padlocks and chains, then heaved the dead bodies out a window. In the process of clearing the floor, he had found the same locked room of horrors that we had, but couldn't do anything with it, other than leave it alone.

As with his barricade, Frank was understandably proud of his arrangements, even now, months later. He had everything he needed for his baby girl, months and months worth of diapers and formula, and he had a fallback plan. But now he could see that food for himself was going to be a problem. With ten apartments in his building, he gathered quite a bit of non-perishable food. But it wouldn't last forever, and now he didn't have any plan or expectation of being rescued, and he had effectively trapped himself in the building.

Water would've been an even more immediate problem, but Frank had found lots of bottles of that electrolyte stuff that they give babies, and there were also quite a few five-gallon water cooler jugs over there, though God only knows how he nimbly skipped across that ladder, carrying a five gallon jug. I would've passed out from fear. He had found a couple soda machines in a nurses' lounge and had taken all the pots and pans from every apartment up to the roof to collect rainwater. All told, he was set for liquid for months, but much less so for food.

"I remembered the first floor of our building was a fancy restaurant," Frank continued. "But how could I get down to it? And if I did, I was pretty sure from watching the dead people come and go out front that they had broken in down there. I had one crazy plan, and if it didn't work, I didn't know what I was going to do. I thought if I got in the very back of the apartment right above the back of the restaurant, *maybe* I could pull up enough floorboards, smash through their ceiling, and make a big enough hole to drop through. Of course, I didn't know the layout of the restaurant, so it'd take a few tries to find their storage room. And all that assumed that when I found it, the storage room wasn't also full of dead people."

"I keep telling Jonah," Jack put in, "the only reason any of us survived is a million little coincidences and lucky breaks. You had your share."

Frank looked thoughtful. And still depressed, but maybe just a little less so. "Yes, I suppose I did. Or it's more like I think that Zoey had hers. I think they were all for Zoey. I didn't want them or ask for them, except for her."

So while his infant daughter slept, Frank got to work on his next insane plan. The dead in the restaurant obviously heard him, but couldn't devise their own plan to kill and eat him, so they just kind of milled around beneath him. "I could hear them as I worked, and when it sounded like there were a lot under me, I'd move to another part of the floor. I was working on a spot, and I hadn't heard any under me. I thought that was good, so I kept trying to get through there.

"Finally, I kicked through the restaurant's ceiling, and one of them grabbed my foot. He was the only one in the room, thank God, and I shook him off. It was a part of the kitchen where all the shelving had fallen across the doorway and kind of trapped him in there. He looked like he worked there—white coat, white pants, like a chef, but all covered in blood. Hell, he's probably still there now."

Before covering up the hole he'd made, Frank had looked through to estimate how far the next wall was, so he could figure where to break through the ceiling again. And when he did, he finally broke into the big storage room with the restaurant's non-perishable food. And it was untouched by the undead. Frank worked quickly and quietly and got everything upstairs without the other restaurant guests ever bothering him. It had been tough on him, but he'd made it and found a way to survive with his daughter.

It was an uplifting, almost inspirational story, but we all knew we couldn't leave it at that. It was another Pandora's box, only this one was now a part of our community, so he had to open up. Maybe only once, and then Jack and I could cover for him and tell people to leave him alone, that he'd been through a lot; but he'd have to tell us, at least. And I'm sure he needed to tell his story, no matter how horrible it was. I was pretty sure Jack was going to make me be the one to ask, so I began. "Frank, was Zoey born right before the outbreak? She looks the right age."

"No, she was born right after. In the apartment." He knew where it was going.

"So your wife was with you in the apartment. You didn't mention her."

He sighed. It was the equivalent of the thousand yard stare, containing all the resignation and regret a human soul could bear, and then that little bit more that it couldn't. Maybe that signal of pain was enough. Maybe I could've told him to forget about it. But we knew that wasn't how it would go. "Yes," he said, "she was, but only for a day after the outbreak."

"What was her name?" I asked, almost in a whisper.

"Mary," he said. It was almost a sob.

We both knew it had to continue. "Frank, what happened to Mary?"

"I don't know if I can tell you. I don't know if I should. Some things are too horrible, even in this world. You'll think I'm crazy. You might even think there's something wrong with Zoey. I don't want that. Blame me. It was all my fault."

"I don't know there is any blame, Frank. We've all done horrible things. I'm sure you know that."

Another sigh. Then he began in earnest. "We were coming back from lunch and looking at baby stuff. We were so happy, and Mary looked so pretty. God, she was so big then, so unbelievably huge, but so pretty. We were almost to the apartment. And this guy in a hospital gown was coming toward us. He had bandages all over him, and he was all bloody. I thought he was a crazy person. He was shoving people out of the way, and it looked like he was snarling at them and lunging at them, but they were just running away and screaming.

"I looked around for a cop or something, but I didn't see anyone. He came closer. I could see then that his eyes weren't right—you know how they look, milky and dead. He grabbed Mary. It was summer, you remember, and she had on a short-sleeved dress. And he sank his teeth into her arm. Oh my God, her scream, it was horrible. And I grabbed him by the throat, to pull him off her, but as I pushed him back, I could see the big chunk of her arm in his teeth, blood gushing down his chin, and I could feel the spray of blood across my face as she spun away from us.

"I held on to him, and he and I fell on the ground. I don't know how, he was a lot bigger than me, but I kept slamming his head into the pavement. I didn't know to do that, of course—I hadn't heard anything about the outbreak yet, or that you had to bash them in the head, but I just did it for some reason."

"Another lucky break for Zoey," Jack said softly. "You got to hold on to that."

Frank nodded. "It was, or he probably would've bitten me too, and then we all would be dead, wandering around out there. When he finally stopped struggling, I went to Mary. I took my shirt off and wrapped her arm, then I took my belt and put on a tourniquet. I had no idea if it was the right way to do it. I hadn't had first aid since we learned it in eighth grade, and then they always told us never to apply a tourniquet unless a limb had been amputated; but the blood was gushing out so badly, with an extra surge with each heartbeat, that I just did it anyway.

"Mary was woozy, but we started toward the hospital. When we got near, I could see more people like the man who'd attacked her. Crazy, snarling people, with hospital personnel and cops fighting with them. And blood everywhere—on them, on the people fighting them, in big puddles on the sidewalk. I'd never seen anything like it. I thought maybe it was some kind of riot or civil war or mass outbreak of insanity, and we should just go inside and wait for things to calm down, and then I could get Mary to the hospital or doctor. So we went into our apartment building."

Being next to the hospital, Frank and his wife were practically at the epicenter of the expanding pandemonium and despair. They watched the television and learned about the plague and the bites. And, of course, Frank's poor wife saw what it meant for her, and what it meant for their baby.

Frank's voice kept getting quieter as he told his story. "She looked at me, pleading, but still in complete control of herself, unlike me. 'Please, whatever you do, don't take off the tourniquet!' I remembered you were supposed to loosen it every few minutes, and never leave it on for hours at a time, or the limb would die and have to be amputated, but I didn't see a choice at that point. I didn't have any idea what to do."

That's when he had started building the barricade on the stairs. It gave him something to do, to feel useful, like he was accomplishing something in the face of all this madness and pain. He still thought he might be able to get his wife out the fire escape and take her to a hospital somewhere, even if the

one next to their building was overrun. Frank shook his head sadly. "I didn't want to have to fight anymore of them. I had no guns or weapons in the apartment. I only found the shotgun later in one of the other apartments. I fell asleep next to Mary on the couch. I hope that I kissed her then, that last night, but I don't remember if I did or not, I was so exhausted.

"When I woke up, I didn't see her. I went to the kitchen. She was sitting at the little table there. She'd made coffee." He looked up, fighting back the tears even as he smiled grimly. "Isn't that funny? I guess she'd gone all those months of being pregnant without it, she really wanted some. And on the table, next to her coffee, was the biggest, sharpest knife we had, with the handle pointed away from her. She was really pale, sweaty, and she was having trouble breathing. 'You're going to have to deliver our baby,' she whispered.

"I still hadn't caught on to what she meant. She wasn't due for two weeks. She pushed the knife toward me, and she talked really slow, over-pronouncing each word. 'Frank, you need to deliver it now, before it turns into . . . before it dies.' I finally got what she was asking. I told her I couldn't just cut her open while she was still alive. I couldn't do that. God, it was too horrible. A person can't just do that."

He stopped a minute before continuing. "Oh God, she was always the decisive one, the logical one. She was so weak from the loss of blood, she was swaying slightly, but she still seemed to be considering what I'd said, and coming up with a solution. 'You're right,' she whispered. 'I understand. But, so we're clear—you promise me that if I die, you'll do anything to save our baby?' I told her of course I would. She nodded, really slowly. Then she snatched up the knife, and jerked it across her throat.

"A stream of blood shot up from her neck, a fountain, so much blood, all the way up the wall; then, as she slumped forward, it gushed out onto the table. I screamed and tried to stop it, but it was obvious she was going to be gone in just a few seconds.

"I held her as she went limp. We were both covered in blood, all hot and sticky, with that metallic smell everywhere. I tried to focus, though, so I picked up the knife. If I didn't know how to apply a tourniquet, how was I going to perform a C-section with a kitchen knife? I was shaking wildly, but I tried cutting her across the belly. I was so nervous and scared I barely broke the skin.

"I screamed like a girl when she grabbed my wrist and lunged for my neck."

Chapter Fourteen

Frank was shaking as he continued. "We were both covered in her blood, so my hand slipped out of her grasp and I staggered back. She tried to come at me again, but the floor was covered with blood, and she slipped and fell. She was growling and moaning. I didn't know what to do. She got to her feet and took a step toward me. But then she stopped.

"She kind of looked up, sort of swaying where she was standing. And sniffing. She was sniffing at the air. Then she looked down at her belly. She put her hands on it, kind of rubbing or patting it, and she gave a low growl, kind of like purring. She'd lost interest in trying to eat me. I had no idea why, at first."

As if what we'd heard already wasn't bad enough, I could unfortunately now guess what was coming. "Oh, no, she didn't," I whispered. But there was no more closing the box. We were going to see it through to the end.

"Yes. She did. She realized there was other prey in the room, much closer than I was. Her fingers went into the gash I'd made in her belly, and she started ripping it open. She peeled the skin back, but then she really had to strain and claw to pull the muscles apart. Blood was gushing up around her hands in thick streams. She was reaching around inside, and then she started pulling out stuff in gobs and flinging it on the floor.

"Finally, her head went back as she got both her hands in there and dug around till she got a hold of our baby. She gave this horrible, animal howl as she ripped it out of herself. Then she was holding it, looking at it, with her mouth hanging open. Its tiny arms and legs were moving as she growled and raised it up to her mouth to eat it.

"I was frozen. I admit it. It wasn't just that I didn't know what to do anymore. I just couldn't think at all. All I could do was watch. But then I heard it cry. Not loud. Kind of just a little squeal, sort of like a kitten would make. And that jolted me out of it.

"I lunged at Mary. I grabbed her hair and jerked her head back, to keep her from biting the baby. I was going to stab her under the chin with the knife, but we both slipped in the blood again. As we fell, her head smashed into the corner of the stove. And it was over. She didn't move anymore.

"I looked around. I'd never seen anything like it. I don't think anyone ever had. The kitchen looked like one of those posters some anti-abortion person would hold up in front of a clinic—blood and fluids and stuff splattered all over. I cut the cord and got Zoey out of there. We were so lucky the water was still running at that point, so I could clean her off. I looked at her, to make sure she wasn't—you know, one of them. She looked fine. But what's going to happen to her? The first thing she saw in the world was her father killing her mother. That isn't right. That can't be good for you."

By this point, both Jack and I were sitting next to him, rubbing his shoulders. "It's okay," Jack said. "You did what you had to. You saved your daughter. Your wife understands.

She's happy with what you did for Zoey. It's going to be okay."

Frank looked at me. I think he'd figured out Jack was the optimistic one, and now he wanted a more sober opinion. I never liked being the bad cop, and especially not in this situation. "What do you think?" he asked me. "I can see that you know there's something wrong with what happened. Tell me the truth."

"There's something wrong with all of us," I said softly, "with everything around us. You can't put the guilt for all that on yourself. I don't even think it's a matter of guilt and innocence anymore. It's a matter of just trying to keep beautiful things alive in an ugly world. And you did that with Zoey. I don't know what else anyone could ask of you at this point."

He shook himself out of it a little, but only to feel guilty about the present rather than the past. "I should be with her. I shouldn't be here drunk. Take me to her."

Jack and I took him to the little room, where we'd left Sarah with little Zoey. Sarah cocked an eyebrow and shook her head at us, with her mock, motherly chastising that she often heaped on us men. We tucked Frank in next to his baby. And although I felt something much more like resignation than optimism, I did feel happy that we had Zoey and Frank here with us. Even though the events Frank had described were ultimately unexplainable and nearly unendurable, the beauty of his daughter and his love for her were as real and as powerful as any of the horrors around us. We would help him to see that, if nothing else.

The following weeks were for Frank what the preceding had been for me. I knew that Jack and Milton had agreed not

to mention the initiation rite to him right away, so he'd have time to adjust to the community. He made friends fairly easily and quickly. It probably helped that Jack and I never told anyone what he had told us that night. We just let him ease into a spot in museum lore: the mysterious man who'd lived the longest in the city of the dead, all the while caring for an infant child.

I don't suppose you ever get over something like Frank had been through, but he definitely seemed to pick up around other people, especially the others who had small children. It's a little embarrassing, but unlike me, Frank actually seemed to like other people's children. He also seemed very much to enjoy working for the community, and whenever he wasn't with Zoey, he was always doing something to help others.

Zoey took to everyone, and of course, everyone loved her. I had never seen such a happy infant, as though her disposition were designed to be the opposite of the horrific events that had surrounded her entrance into this veil of tears. She took her first steps as I watched. She played with other babies for the first time in her life. I think Tanya knew that Popcorn would not tolerate any perceived threat to the attention she showed him, so she didn't dote on the baby particularly, but Sarah had no such qualms and was with Zoey constantly. It seemed to brighten her up immensely, and I was glad for her. Jack was maybe a little less so, but he was more than good-natured enough to make it into a joke: he said if he kept doing Sarah like he had been, she'd soon have one of her own.

The Fourth of July came, and Milton again snuck out, as he had told me he had at Christmas, to try to make things a little special for us. Just some noisemakers and sparklers from a party store, but it certainly brightened up the sultry, summer night. And our garden had yielded some small watermelons for us to share that evening. Even the dead seemed just lazy and not so belligerent under the hot and dry skies. Most days, Milton would just go out and shoo them away from our gates and into the cool shadows of the park across the street, rather than sending out people to try and kill them. It was shaping up to be a good summer, all things considered.

But we knew there would soon be another mission outside the compound to check out the smoke I had seen when we got the helicopter. Evidence of more survivors immediately raised Jack's feelings of responsibility—he had to help them as he had helped all the people he'd already brought into the community. And, as with so many other things, there was the overwhelming power of curiosity; once you knew there were survivors just a few miles away, you had to see who they were.

I understood all that, but I began to wonder if maybe we had enough people here, and we needed to focus on helping them, and building up what we had, rather than trying to find others. We couldn't save or rebuild the whole world, after all. But in the end, this was all neither here nor there, for I knew I would back whatever plan Jack came up with. It wasn't his grandstanding or charisma or even his logic; it was just the gratitude most everyone in the community showed him for saving all of our lives at various times.

Based on the situations they'd rescued people from previously, Jack wanted to take just a small group: big enough to break through a few besieging zombies if we found survivors barricaded in some building, but not enough to use up extra fuel with more than one vehicle, or to weaken the defenses at the museum. Tanya wanted to go, mostly to kill more zombies, and I wanted to go, both to help Jack, and, I had to admit, to be by Tanya. As kind of an old-school soldier, Jack certainly frowned on the latter motive, but he also understood it was going to be nearly unavoidable in the very small, domestic army he'd assembled here.

Popcorn wanted to go for a combination of the motives of Tanya and myself—to kill more zombies, and to be near Tanya. If it had seemed like a more dangerous mission, Jack would surely have objected to him coming, but by that time, Popcorn had been on a couple of their raids for food, as well as the raid to the local airport to get fuel for the helicopter.

As the only pilot, Franny was ineligible for missions until she could train someone else.

Finally, Frank wanted to go, and Jack welcomed the opportunity to make him feel more a part of the community, even if technically he had not been through the initiation rite.

We took a smaller vehicle, a jeep that belonged to another person in the museum community. This would be farther than anyone had ever ventured from the museum, so we left early. The plan was to circle way to the north before turning west, avoiding the city proper entirely. We weren't optimistic about finding anything on the first try. We didn't know exactly where we should look, so we'd need to see the smoke again to zero in on them. In the heat of summer, it seemed unlikely that they'd be burning fires all the time, so we hoped that, if we left early enough, their fire from the previous evening's meal would still be smoldering in the early morning light.

Sure enough, that is what we saw as we weaved between abandoned cars on one of the roads north of town—a barely visible line of white trailing up to a long, faint smudge where a breeze had spread it during the night and early morning.

I watched Jack's face as he drove us closer to it. He was

so laughably easy to read. It was obvious that he thought something was not quite right about the location. When we were close, he turned off the main road, down a side road, and across a field, till we were way out in the middle of the field, next to some scraggly saplings at the base of an electrical tower that rose high above us.

From here we had a good view for a long ways around, and saw no movement of any kind. I noticed the saplings and the bushes would hide the jeep from view, and that there was a hill between us and the source of the smoke. "Let's park it here and scout around before we go driving up," Jack said, trying to act nonchalant about it; I could tell there was a change of plans by what he said. "They ought to be just over that rise, whoever they are."

"You don't want them to know that we have a vehicle?" I asked as we got out of the jeep.

Jack looked at me sideways. "We don't know the situation. I don't want to advertise that we're here until we do. Normal tactical decision."

I remembered Jack's comments about the anti-tank missiles being better suited for use against other people than against the undead, and I sensed that this was a strategic, and not a tactical decision. But I let it drop in front of the others. We were still pretty far away from whatever it was. It couldn't do any harm to walk over the hill and check it out. There was a stand of trees a hundred feet to our left, and another way off to the right, but otherwise we were in the clear and could see any trouble with plenty of time to react or flee.

As we walked through the tall grass, I looked back and saw that Jack's parking job had in fact hidden the jeep, as I had thought it would. We came up and over the brow of the next hill and could finally see, maybe a little less than a mile ahead of us, at the top of another, lower hill, the source of the smoke. It was coming from a large building behind a high, gray wall, several stories tall. The wall also enclosed a water tower and some smaller buildings. The wall was surrounded by two enormous rectangles of cyclone fencing, both topped with razor wire.

"The regional correctional facility," Jack said. "I saw the signs on the main road as we got close. Our new neighbors."

We walked a few more yards downhill toward the prison to get a better view. "The gate must be on the other side," Jack said as he scanned with the binoculars. "I don't see any movement."

"Nice people being eaten alive, and some bunch of rapists and perverts gets to ride it out in style in a fortress I helped pay for," Tanya said with disgust, absentmindedly chopping at the grass with her machete. I'd never thought of discussing politics with her, as it seemed pretty moot by the time I met her, but I could see she was going to be a little to the right of most of my college professor friends. That didn't seem all that bad to me at this point.

I heard a whistling sound, then a thwack, and then Jack cried out in pain—an arrow stuck in his left shoulder. Another thwack, and he staggered with a second arrow in his left thigh.

I raised my pistol, but I could see nothing among the shadows in the trees, and then I felt a shooting pain in my right chest as an arrow hit me.

"Drop your damn guns," a voice came to us from the shadows.

"Jack?" I asked, not wanting to be the one to surrender, still scanning the trees for a target.

"You got to," Jack rasped. "We can't see them, we can't shoot back, you got to."

Jack dropped his pistol and raised his right arm, and his left arm part of the way, in surrender. I dropped my pistol and raised my arms, and the others did as well.

Nine men emerged from the trees. All carried various hand-to-hand weapons like clubs and knives, as well as homemade bows. All were stripped to the waist. Most were covered with tattoos. What seemed to be their leader, a tall black man, picked up our firearms. The others hung back and kept their arrows trained on us.

"Who are you?" the black man asked.

"We were just out foraging for supplies, and we saw the smoke and followed it here," Jack wheezed.

"Where are you from?"

"There's a bunch of us holed up in a compound to the west," Jack said, lying about our location.

"Well, you're not going back there today," the leader said. "You four, get going. That way." He pointed off to the right and toward the prison.

"What about him?" asked one of the other men, pointing at Jack.

"He can't move fast enough. Leave him." The black man bent down and twisted the arrow that was still in Jack's thigh. Jack winced and gritted his teeth through the pain. "If you do hobble your sorry ass back home, tell them not to mess with us." He got up and turned to the others in his group. "Get the deer and stuff," he said, and four of the others went back to the trees. When they emerged, they were carrying two deer, suspended by their feet from two long poles. Another pair of men went back and returned with large bundles of firewood.

They made us walk along ahead of them. I managed to pull the arrow out of my chest, and I could apply pressure to the wound as I walked, so I wouldn't lose too much blood. The arrow was rudimentary—no real arrowhead, just a sharpened wooden shaft, so it didn't have any barb that would tear a bigger hole when I pulled it out.

We walked along for twenty minutes, circling to the right, and they made us stop by a big drainage pipe that stuck out of the hillside under the prison. It was concrete, about four feet in diameter, and it had a metal grate across it. A stream of dirty water ran out of it and down the side of the hill.

The leader approached the grate and unlocked it. He swung it up and held it open. "Get in there," he commanded.

I got in first and started crawling along. It was foul, and after the first minute, it was completely dark. I had no idea how they managed to pull the deer along behind us, but I assumed they had done this before and were good at it.

After a while, I saw some light up ahead. When I got to it, I could see that someone had dug through and smashed into the pipe from above. I stood up through the opening, so that my eyes were at about ground level, even with the edge of the hole that they had dug down into the pipe. I was surrounded by men like those who had captured us, and I immediately heard their catcalls: "Good hunting! Fresh meat!"

They pulled me out of the hole, followed by Tanya, Popcorn, and Frank. The catcalls got really loud when the second two emerged. I shivered. Ironically, months of dealing with only non-human monsters had made us soft and naïve. We had forgotten about the ugliness and brutality that humans could so gleefully perpetrate on anyone weaker than themselves, imagining that ours was the worst possible hell, when we should've remembered that it wasn't. Not even close.

When our captors climbed out with their other prizes, they led us across the field into which we had emerged. We were behind the walls of the prison proper, but not in the building itself, to which we were now being led. Most of the field here had been planted with corn, which seemed to be doing well. Not being a farmer, I forgot if, by the Fourth of July, corn was supposed to be as high as your eye, or knee-high. This looked somewhere in between.

I guessed that the drainage pipe had really been an old stream that had been buried when the prison was built. It carried water down from the hills above, and supplemented it with the prison's filth before dumping it out where we came in. If the inmates had tapped into it, they'd have some water to stay alive and to cultivate their new crops.

As we walked toward the large gray building, we stopped at a basketball court under the baking sun. The macadam of several other courts had been smashed up and hauled away to make room for more corn; the hoops still stuck out, incongruously, above the crops. But this court remained blacktop, though it had plenty of cracks with weeds growing out of them. The men hoisted the two deer up by their hind legs, suspending them from the backboards.

"Better get started on these quick in this heat," the leader shouted to some other men who were just lolling about, staring at us.

"I could get a good price for you all out here, but I guess I got to take you to meet the man," the leader of the group said as we continued walking.

"Who's that?" Tanya risked asking.

"Coppertop," the leader replied. "That's what the brothers call him. He calls himself Copperhead—some big, damn snake from the south, where his big, dumb, redneck ass is from. Thinks he's all bad and shit."

"And he's not?" I asked.

He shoved me on my right side, and pain shot through me from the arrow wound. "Oh, I think we're all plenty bad enough for you, little man. Now keep moving and shut up. 'Nuff of your stupid questions."

We entered the main building and went through some areas that had obviously been checkpoints and entrances when the place had functioned as a prison; there were doors of bulletproof glass operated by electrical switches, where people had to be buzzed through, watched over by guardrooms with speakers and control panels. Now everything was just a smashed-up mess, and you stepped through the doors where the glass would've been.

Where there was enough light from the windows, weeds grew in the cracks in the floor. The prisoners hadn't really bothered to sweep up the bits and pieces of glass from whenever this attack had taken place—which I suspected was soon after the zombie crisis had begun—but had just left them everywhere; over the months, they had been pulverized into a fine, sparkly dust where people walked regularly.

Past these, we were into the main cell block. It looked like an old prison, with four floors of cells facing a central, open area. The roof had a row of large skylights down the middle.

Not as organized or tidy as the people in the museum, the prisoners had nonetheless taken similar precautions against an undead break-in: they had demolished the concrete stairs where they led up from the ground floor to the second tier, so the zombies couldn't get up. It looked crude, as though they had smashed the concrete with a sledgehammer, then cut through the rebar somehow and curled it back like some weird, big plant or hairdo.

The catcalls here increased, though it was obvious as I looked up at the leering faces that there weren't that many men living here, probably only a few dozen, in a place designed to hold hundreds. We climbed a rope ladder to the second tier, then walked from there up to the fourth and topmost one.

We were led to a cell. The one wall had been knocked out to connect it to the adjacent chamber, and part of the roof and outside wall had been smashed out as well, all with the same careless demolition as the stairs and the pipe and the basketball courts, leaving dusty, crumbling holes with rusting rebar curling back like the eyelashes of giant Cyclopes. The hole let a breeze through in the heat of summer, and the room was much cooler and more comfortable than those on the lower tiers.

All over the room sat large, one-gallon cans labeled "PEACHES" and "PEARS," and the room reeked of rotted fruit and yeasty fermentation, like a brewery or an ethanol plant. The walls were covered with pretty typical pornographic pictures, though there was a definite preference for blondes. A few firearms leaned on the walls and sat on the floor. To these, the black man who had captured us now added our guns. The entire floor was covered with deer skins. These guys must've lived on nothing but venison. For some reason, I suspected that it was barely cooked, too.

In the midst of all these bizarre and hyper-masculine furnishings sat what I took to be Copperhead, a large, bald white man covered with tattoos, all of which were some combination of the Confederate flag, naked women, snakes, and flames. I remembered that Queequeg's tattoos were supposed to reveal the secret meaning of the universe. I felt sure that this guy's revealed the rather straightforward meaning of his own base urges and desires. And I was very sure that it would've been much better for everyone—himself included—if he had kept them secret.

He saw me looking at the fruit cans and grinned. "Good old-fashioned pruno!" he crowed. "Best we can do—so far! I like to keep it close, or the boys'll be stealing me blind. Still is a might hard to take, but we're working on the recipe. Got some boys out back, working on a still—that ought to smooth it out real good, 'cause it's all the rot from the fruit that makes it nasty. And when that corn comes in—could be some corn whiskey, I'm hoping! That, plus the big tractor-trailer full of cigarettes we found turned over on the interstate—we'll be set!"

Great. Our final days of being sodomized and beaten to death were going to be overseen by Boss Hogg's insane, inbred nephew. I'd been hoping for someone a little more Mephistophelean, but if the zombies had taught us one thing, it was that you don't get to pick your apocalypses or your devils—they pick you.

"Couldn't you go out and find some regular booze?" I asked, without even thinking of the danger of seeming disrespectful and incurring some physical punishment for it.

Copperhead apparently didn't think the question was impertinent, but just that it was kind of silly. "No, 'cause then we'd need cars and shit."

"You could get them from the interstate. You said you were by the interstate."

"Yeah, but then we'd have to have somebody guard the gate when they go out, and open it up when they come back, and fight all those dead assholes, and find gas! It's the same reason we only have a couple guns here, the ones we took from the guards—you can't just go out and get more!"

He announced it in triumph, as though he'd found some fatal flaw in a plan that required only the barest of forethought and effort to make it work. He—and, I take it, the others, since they went along with it—would rather drink something that smelled like a dumpster than make the effort to get something else. It would be hilarious if I didn't know this guy and his colleagues planned to rape and kill all of us. I let the matter drop. No sense hastening the process.

The tall black man who'd captured us explained how they had found us. Copperhead got up to inspect us, nodding approvingly. "Now that's nice, that's real nice, having company. We done just about used up all the old guards, hadn't we? Now we got us a whole fresh batch for the Pit! Oh, that's where you'll be staying when you're with us—it's what we call the first floor of our little home."

His attention and nodding lingered especially over Tanya. "Now, isn't this a fine-looking gal we got here?" He put his hand on her hip and slipped it around to caress his buttocks. "Yeah, I might have to breed you, you look so fine, and not get out the old coat hanger like we did when we knocked up those guard bitches."

"Killed three of them that way," the tall black man muttered.

"Yeah," Copperhead said ruefully. "We should've been

more careful, but we didn't want any brats running around here, messing things up." He went back to fondling Tanya, this time moving up to her breasts. "You know, my daddy wouldn't have approved, you being a nigger and all." He leaned close to lick her ear, whispering now. "That's not why I killed him with that hammer, of course. But still, I never believed all that racist bullshit, did you?"

Tanya knew enough not to say anything belligerent, if for no other reason than that she didn't want Popcorn to see her raped and killed. But she also couldn't bring herself to say anything that was appropriately friendly.

Copperhead slid down her body, blowing kisses at her breasts and crotch as his flunkies cheered him on. Slowly, he brought his right hand across to his left hip, then he uncoiled and viciously backhanded her across the face. Popcorn, Frank, and I couldn't help but take a step forward, but there were hands all over us, and knives stuck in our faces almost before we'd moved. Copperhead showed he wasn't at all lazy when it came to meting out pain and degradation.

As Tanya staggered back from the blow, he grabbed her by the throat and slammed her into the wall with his right hand, as his left hand grabbed her crotch. "You're gonna learn to be a nice nigger, little missy," he hissed, "for me and any other ugly-ass hump that has a pack of cigarettes to pay the Pit crew. The only choice you got is whether you learn easy, or hard."

He turned to his helpers. "You tell them to keep the boys away from this one for a while. I'll catch up with her later on. I don't think she's had a real man for a while." He sneered at me and Frank.

Copperhead let Tanya down and returned to his jovial, good ole boy routine. "But not tonight," he said expansively. "I say that tonight's the Fourth of July! Must be some time about now! Y'all have a calendar where you come from?" he asked, turning to me.

I shook my head and shrugged. No sense ruining a twenty-four hour reprieve.

"Yep—that settles it! It's tonight! And it'd be disrespectful to the good ole U. S. of A. to be carrying on like cats in heat when we should be showing our gratitude to this great country, what built us this fine, zombie-proof castle to live in and drink our fine hooch, and smoke all that fine tobacco, and thank God for our *freedom*!" A little cheer went up from his flunkies.

He turned to Popcorn. "Except we really can't have *no* cavorting tonight. I'm sorry, son," he said with an icy, horrifying mock sadness and crocodile tears, shaking his head slowly. "No, we've never had a young 'un in here. And, you know, some of the boys here—well, we don't know exactly why," his eyes went heavenward and he really did seem to get dreamy and thoughtful, though I'd already seen that he was equal parts sadism and playacting, "but the good Lord gave them this powerful hunger for a special, little friend. And some of them been living with that hunger for years and years in here, with no way to satisfy it."

He patted Popcorn on the cheek, and I could see the fear and anger in the boy's eyes that he'd never shown, even when he was surrounded by ghouls who would kill and eat him alive.

"And, son," Copperhead said, "you can help them with that—isn't that nice? Well, you can help the ones of them that would pay dearly for it." He turned back to his followers and went back to the jovial routine. "Because let's not forget, boys, the business of America—is business!" Another little cheer went up, this time with a chuckle.

We were led away to our cells in the Pit, to await the festivities and horrors that their Fourth of July celebration would bring us. I had met the self-styled ruler of this hell, and he was a gruesome, swollen, little clown who thought he could dictate orders to time itself. God knows how much damage he could do if he weren't so damned lazy and stupid. But the damage he could do to the four of us would be more than satisfying enough to his stunted, twisted mind, and more than our exhausted, ill-fed bodies could endure.

Like Sarah in her dentist's office, I found myself only hoping it would be quick, but doubting this time that it would be. The dead were capable of such a meager mercy, but I was sure that such living monsters were not.

Chapter Fifteen

THEY STUCK TANYA, Frank, and me in three adjacent cells, near the end of the block farthest from the entrance. Across from us were Popcorn and the last two guards they hadn't worked or raped to death. They were a man and a woman, and from what I could see, they both looked pretty listless. They probably welcomed our arrival, as we would now absorb some of the physical abuse, but they looked too worn out to register anything.

The doors to the cells couldn't be closed, I assume because the power was off. Actually, I don't know if they really were stuck open, or if the inmates were just too lazy to bother closing them manually. Regardless, it meant there was a rather sizeable number of men—what Copperhead had somewhat predictably referred to as the "Pit crew"—to guard us constantly. They were armed with pieces of rebar, knives, and clubs, but I saw that no bows were allowed below the second tier, and no one had firearms outside of Copperhead's cell. I assumed they were imitating the rules that had been in force when the place was a regular prison—guards were not allowed guns when among the prisoners, lest one of the prisoners get a hold of a gun.

I also suspected that the Pit crew were of low social

standing, for they seemed slightly more depraved even than the rest of the inmates—scrawny, cowering little creatures, more interested in the financial gain that could be gotten from physical cruelty, rather than the actual inflicting of it. Pimps and panderers, in the old-fashioned meanings of those words. They were probably next in line for rape and abuse, should the bottommost rung of their society ever run out.

Still, there were probably more than enough of them to beat us to death, should we ever try to fight back.

I sat in my cell with such thoughts, sullen and glowering. I thought of improvising a weapon, but didn't have the right kind of imagination for such handiwork. They had left us with nothing but our clothes, and the cell was utterly bare, beyond a filthy mattress and a non-functioning metal toilet and sink built into the wall. I also had no idea how to come up with any kind of plan for escape.

I thought that it might be possible that Jack might have made it back to the museum. But even if he had, it would take him some time to drive a stick shift back with his left leg hurt. And I also couldn't estimate how long it would take him to coordinate an attack on the prison, or how they would even be able to go about it. The people at the museum were set up for defense, not for mounting massive assaults on fixed positions. And they were used to fighting zombies, not this band of crazed sadists, armed with bows and guns.

And how much would Jack risk to save the four of us, who, for all he knew, were already dead? I knew him well, and we were good friends, I thought, but I also knew how logical he was, and how much he valued the community over any individual.

After a few hours, the odor of roasting flesh filled the prison. I have to admit, it was the one aspect of the prisoners'

communal life that I found far preferable to that of our people.

We were taken outside by the basketball court, where the two deer were suspended on spits over a fire pit. Their heads were obscenely displayed on stakes stuck in the ground nearby—wide-eyed and tongues lolling out.

Copperhead emerged from the building and moved through the crowd to great acclimation for his magnanimity—not that any of them would've known to call it that. Two of his flunkies walked behind him, carrying a huge pot of the hideous fruit liquor, Copperhead's generous offering to his faithful subjects.

He cut the tongue out of one deer head and roasted it himself on the end of a knife, making a big show out of suspending it lewdly above his mouth and licking it before devouring it, bloody grease dripping down his chin. A cheer went up, and he raised his hands to speak.

"That's how I'm gonna do this fine sister tomorrow night!"

A bigger cheer went up.

"But don't you worry—every man who can afford it will have his turn, once I break that fine ass in! It ain't like the old days—race don't make no difference here!"

There was another big cheer.

"But tonight, boys, enjoy this feast! It's the Fourth of July! God bless America!" He gave a mocking salute to the barely recognizable, tattered flag that still flew on the flagpole outside. The biggest cheer of all rose up, from a bunch of goons who I felt sure had never celebrated the Fourth in any normal way since childhood, and who were now free to indulge their own sadistic, hedonistic version of freedom to their sick hearts' content. The whole scene made *The Lord of the Flies* look like *Little Women.*

After Copperhead kicked off the festivities, we were treated to the spectacle of men devouring as much bloody flesh as they could. Like animals in the wild, they ate in descending rank. Copperhead ate first, like the leading male lion of the pride—even though, exactly like the chief male lion, he had done none of the work of procuring the feast.

Then it was the turn of the other lions of the pride: Copperhead's immediate henchmen and those from the hunting party, who lived on the prison's topmost tier, called "Park Avenue." Those others who lived on the second and third tiers—which I learned were called "Uptown" and "Downtown," respectively—came next, like the hyenas that descend on the lions' kill. Then the Pit crew was allowed to eat, like jackals, not wanting to offend or anger the more dangerous carnivores.

Finally, when there was no danger and all had torn off their share, the six of us who were the prisoners of the Pit were allowed to feed, like vultures, from the most unsavory scraps.

Starved as I was, in the presence of the first cooked meat I'd smelled in nearly a year, the barbaric feast tasted like the best thing I'd ever eaten, as I'm sure it did to the others as well. Gnawing on a bone as I looked at the inmates lolling about in a blood- and meat-gorged stupor, I again thought of how frighteningly little separated us from the other carnivores, staggering about outside the prison, with stupefied looks on their still-human faces.

Sitting on the ground in the twilight, once our hunger was sated, all we could feel was complete dread and helplessness at what was to come. And what could we say, especially to Popcorn? "I'm sorry," was far too meager and vague, while, "It'll be okay," was a lie. "Don't worry—it'll be our turn tomorrow night," was probably the most grimly honest, but wouldn't offer much consolation to him or us. Assuring him that we would fight would be true, up to a point. But we all knew eventually we'd have to stop and let it happen, or we'd be beaten to death, and then it would happen anyway.

Oddly, it was Frank who spoke up; he'd been silent almost since we left the museum that morning, which seemed a lifetime ago. "I think you guys are going to make it," he said. "And when you do, take care of Zoey for me. Tell her how much her mom and I loved her."

I think right then, we might have thought it was a little callous of him—making the situation about him, when it was obviously Popcorn who was going to suffer the most, at least that night. But Frank rubbed Popcorn's shoulder, and we just took his words to be an awkward expression of hopefulness for us. And for one of the few times I'd ever seen, Popcorn let someone other than Tanya express tenderness for him, so perhaps he knew what Frank meant, even if those of us who were older and supposedly wiser did not.

They rounded us up at that point and took us back inside. The men who lived in the tiers above ascended their ladders, and the Pit crew was now more vigilant in guarding us in our separate cells. Torches were burning, and the light from a nearly-full moon shined through the skylights, making it possible to see a little in the gloom of the Pit.

They tried to conduct things as quietly as possible, maybe out of some slight fear of unnecessarily provoking us to violence, maybe out of some tiny shred of vestigial humanity and shame at what they were about to do to an innocent child. I suppose they would've said they were being civilized or merciful about it, but words lose all meaning when stretched to such grotesque extremes.

A man came down the rope ladder to be Popcorn's first visitor. He went in the cell, with two guards watching from outside. One guard was standing right outside the door of each of our cells, with more in reserve. I stood up, and I'm sure Frank and Tanya did the same.

The guard at my cell door half raised a piece of rebar and growled. "Sit down before I bust you all up. I don't want to ruin that pretty face before I make you my bitch."

There were any number of witty repartees I could make at that point, but now was not the time. The only one I allowed myself was to think that, after a year of privation, I most definitely was *not* pretty, no matter in what direction one's tastes ran.

If the three of us rushed our guards at the same time, we could probably get past them. And if we got a weapon away from each of them, we could maybe take out a couple more. Then the rest would beat us to death. Popcorn's inhuman degradation would be postponed maybe ten minutes.

Still, you had to make sacrifices for the payoff that was offered. We all can't die on Omaha beach, winning back freedom for millions of people. Some of us die on a filthy prison floor to defend a little boy, even though it won't make the slightest difference to what happens to him.

As I clenched my fists at my side and took a step forward, I knew how lucky I was. Some people died for nothing at all. I was going to die, smashing this ugly bastard's head into the floor and taking that piece of rebar from him, so I could smash a couple more ugly bastards' heads into pulp. That counted for a lot, in my book; and unless God was a much bigger asshole than I thought, part of me felt sure it counted for something with Him.

Chapter Sixteen

But the guard and I were both stopped, before either could attack, by a hideous scream coming from Popcorn's cell. Some small, wet object landed with a splat on the floor outside the cell, and the man emerged, clutching at his face. "By doze! Son of a bitch bit by doze!"

There was a guffaw from the crowd assembled on the second tier, who had come out to see what the commotion was. The two guards went into Popcorn's cell; one pushed the bitten man out of the way. "You dumb bitch! Can't even do a kid without help?!"

There was more scuffling and yelling in the cell, and more guards went in. I never heard Popcorn's voice, only those of the men he viciously fought. But after a minute, it was still except for the dull thuds of fists hitting a body that wasn't moving or fighting back, but just being methodically pummeled into a bloody, submissive lump. Frank shouted, "Stop! You can't do that!" He charged his guard and tackled him. It distracted my guard for an instant, and I jumped on him, knocking him down.

I got his right arm—the one holding the rebar—pinned to the floor as I punched him in the face with my other hand. His grip slackened on the rebar, and I grabbed it. I raised it up to

smash him in the face, but two other guys grabbed me from behind and pulled me to my feet.

I was still struggling, but it was useless at this point. Somewhere in the partial darkness above us, Copperhead shouted, "Go help those assholes in the Pit!"

He sent more men down the rope ladders from the second tier to help the Pit crew beat us into submission. I could see to my left that they had Tanya restrained similarly to how they had me.

The guard I had originally knocked down was back up. He kicked me in the testicles, then punched me in the face. I could taste blood, my ears were ringing, and spots were exploding before my eyes.

I roared, tore my left hand free, and tried to hit the guy holding my right arm, but my guard pinned my free arm behind me while another guy punched me in the stomach, then two more times in the face.

Now I could barely hear or see anything; my mouth hung slack to let out a steady stream of blood, and I wasn't able to draw in breath with the wind knocked out of me. I stopped struggling. It was a reflex. You couldn't will to go on with that kind of pain overwhelming you.

Well, I couldn't. Some of us are made of sterner stuff, under the right circumstances. And that night, it was Frank, for some reason. He threw off one of the Pit crew and grabbed the guy's knife. He slashed the man across the face, causing him to scream and fall back. Frank kept slashing as he yelled, "You can't do that! You can't! Leave him alone!"

The Pit crew hung back, afraid of getting cut.

I could see now why he had told us to take care of Zoey. It was because he'd had enough, and he knew he was going

to die defending Popcorn. I should've seen earlier that he'd reached his own breaking point and was having his own thousand yard stare. Fighting zombies, killing his own wife, living on starvation rations for ten months—he'd somehow managed to survive all that for Zoey's sake.

But ironically, being safe with us had made him less able to carry on in the face of absurd and dehumanizing cruelty; he knew Zoey would be taken care of, so why should he turn his back on Popcorn's suffering and try to survive himself? I tried to yell, "No, Frank!" but I don't know what came out. Probably just a gurgling sound from a mouth full of blood.

Then there was that whistling and thwack sound as an arrow sank into Frank's back. He groaned and staggered. One of them tried to grab him, but he slashed again, and blood flew off of the guy's hand. There was another thwack, and Frank was hit with an arrow from the front. He staggered and finally fell.

The Pit crew descended on him like the cowardly, herd beasts that they were, brutally kicking and beating him. As in Popcorn's cell, after the first couple of blows, there was no sound or sign of any struggle, but just the terrible thuds of fists and feet hitting over and over.

They finally pulled him up, and he was covered from the waist up in blood. The spots around the broken shafts of the arrows were now no redder than the rest of him. Both his eyes were swollen shut, and his mouth hung open, dribbling blood. He could barely cough to clear his throat and draw in a wheezing breath through all the fluid.

One of the Pit crew yelled up into the darkness, "Copperhead, you sure we need both of these new bitch-boys? This one's a pain in the ass!"

"Can't you assholes do anything right?" Copperhead

replied. "I bring you new toys, and you just screw it up!" There was a pause, then finally he said, "No, I guess we don't need both."

The jackals in the Pit seemed to like that. Now they could inflict pain not just for profit, and not even out of fear and rage. Now they could just be cruel for its own sake, as they had probably seen done so often by this hellhole's elite, either before or after the inmates took over.

Holding out Frank's arms, they tied his wrists to the bars of the cell door. Tanya and I were, of course, made to watch.

The two men whom Frank had cut were allowed to visit some special indignity or pain upon him for their troubles. The first took back the knife and put it beside Frank's head. "Son of a bitch cut my face!" he yelled. "I'll take something off your face!"

His arm moved back and forth in a sawing motion, and a cascade of blood fell at Frank's feet. He let out a gurgling scream.

Finished, the guy held up Frank's severed right ear. He slashed downward across Frank's face to punctuate his point. "Gonna wear it around my neck on a string when I do that brat kid you cut me over! Gonna do him twice as hard when I think of you, you crazy, dumb bastard!" The crowds on the second tier cheered.

The second guy took the knife and yelled, "This crazy asshole cut my hand!" And he stabbed Frank's right hand, driving the blade all the way through it. Frank screamed again, writhing against his bonds. The guy then walked over and did the same to his left hand. Again the crowd roared its approval.

We waited a moment, I guess to let Frank suffer more. It was deathly silent—unnaturally and painfully silent. You could just hear the animal panting of all of us, the throb of life, the life that inevitably craves another's death and suffering. The throbbing seemed to fill my head, seeping up through the floor into me, but then it became audible as the crowd on the second tier started chanting, "Kill! Kill! Kill!"

Given how Frank looked, I almost welcomed the chant of bloodlust, to hasten an end to his pain. One of the Pit crew walked up with a spear and stabbed Frank in the side with it. More blood gushed out, running down to puddle on the floor. I could never quite visualize until that night just how much blood is in the human body. The undead were usually a dry and crusty lot, or they exploded with puss and putrefaction: only a living body could spill out the incredible affluence of thick, rich, beautiful and horrifying blood. Frank was almost too weak to move at this point, but only flinched slightly at this final blow. The crowd gave another cheer.

"Will you numb nuts make sure he doesn't get back up again, please?" Copperhead asked the Pit crew.

Another member came up with a wooden baseball bat with enormous nails driven through it. I looked away, but I could hear the sickening glitch and crunch as he slammed it into Frank's head. It was finished. One of the most courageous men I had ever known—a man who had surely suffered enough already—had died, utterly forsaken and in agony.

"Let them take him down and bury him," Copperhead directed from above. "Oh—and if they're going to bury him, I guess they're going to use shovels?"

"Well, yeah, sure," one of the Pit crew replied.

"And what are shovels good for?" Copperhead asked.

The fellow hadn't caught Copperhead's sarcasm. "Uh, digging holes?"

"Yes—and hitting dumb asses in the head! So make sure they're guarded better this time!"

Speaking for myself, Copperhead needn't have worried too much. I could barely walk, breathe, see, or hear. I doubt I was much of a threat at that point.

Tanya and I got Frank's body down and dragged it outside with difficulty. We were accompanied by four guards, who gave us the shovels after we had set Frank's body down. We worked slowly, digging, sometimes almost hacking, through the dense, hard, red clay. The guards didn't seem to care if it took us awhile, as they were well supplied with the vile fruit liquor.

If I hadn't been busted up so bad, we might have entertained thoughts of attacking them, they were obviously getting so inebriated. But as it was, they sat around, laughing and not paying much attention to us. I also saw, lurking in the background, the large black man who had captured us that morning. I presumed he was there to make sure that Tanya was kept intact for Copperhead.

When we were down to a good depth of about four feet, Tanya and I stopped. It wasn't the official six feet, but we were exhausted.

We climbed out and heaved Frank's body into the hole. They hadn't given us anything with which to wrap or cover him, and he landed in a particularly grotesque and awkward pose, with his arms outstretched above him, his legs bent up under him, and the hideous nail hole in his forehead clearly visible, blood obscuring his whole face.

"Poor son of a bitch," Tanya said. "Can't leave him like that." She jumped back into the hole. Again, it simply was not in her just to ignore—as I would've been inclined to—something as emotionally weighty but physically inconsequential as a person's final posture in the grave.

She straightened his legs out and folded his hands across his chest. Then she raked some of his hair down across his bloody face and turned his head to the right, covering the bloody hole where his ear had been and hiding the nail hole in his forehead. While it was definitely an improvement, the extent of Frank's stigmata made it impossible to do too much. I shook my head at Tanya's kind and loving attempts, knowing that back in the normal world, this would most definitely be a closed casket affair.

I helped her climb out, and we stood there a moment. "They led him like a lamb to the slaughter," I half-sobbed, half-gurgled through my own blood and rising tears. I had no idea why, as I looked down at Frank's broken, humiliated body, I would remember that imagery from a biblical verse. I didn't even remember where it was from in the Bible. I guess it was supposed to mean Jesus, but I wasn't sure.

"They sure did," she agreed. "Poor guy toughs it out for months against the living dead, and these assholes kill him in less than a day. It's not right." She looked at me and asked, "You know the next verse?"

"What? After the one I said? No, I have no idea."

"What, you just sort of remembered it from *Silence of the Lambs*?" she sneered. Then she lifted her eyes to the warm, dark sky, her hands at her sides, palms forward. "O Lord of hosts, that judgest righteously, let me see thy vengeance on them."

Leave it to the spiritually profound Tanya to remember a verse that I could pray without hesitation. I repeated it over and over in my mind as we picked up our shovels and proceeded to fling the damp, dead clods onto Frank's body.

Chapter Seventeen

When we went back inside, Popcorn's cell was pretty much walled off from our view by guards, I assume to prevent further trouble from us. Tanya and I were led to our respective cells. I sat there, looking across at the shadows moving on the other side of the cell block, straining to hear anything, but I could detect nothing. We all knew what was going on. But there was nothing we could do at this point.

I slept fitfully sitting up. Close to dawn, I could hear one of the guards whisper to Tanya, "Hey, bitch, go over and sit with the kid. He needs you." I saw her walk over, then I dozed back off.

In the early morning light, I looked over again. The guards had dispersed at some point in the night, and I could see Tanya and Popcorn clearly. They both were asleep. Tanya was sitting ... ng leaning against the back wall of the cell, like I was. He was across her lap, on his side, turned slightly toward me.

As the light grew brighter, I could see them more ... nctly. The way they were sitting, the morning light act... shined brightly across them. Popcorn was in as bad a s... s I had imagined he would be—bruised and bloodied f... d to toe, lips cut and swollen, one eye swollen shut. Th... ological or

spiritual wounds that I couldn't see were probably much worse. Bathed in the morning light, his brutalized body graceful now and still, her beautiful and loving face bent toward him, both of them suffused with the peace of sleep and the vivifying glow of the sun—they could not have looked more like a pietà if they had deliberately staged it.

After a while, the prison began to stir with the more mundane and profane forms of life that dwelt in it. Eventually, we were led outside to stretch and spend some time in the light and fresh air.

While passing through the shattered remains of the guard room and entrance in order to go outside, Popcorn tripped on the doorframe and fell sideways, onto the floor of the control room. I reached down for him, but he batted away my hand. He scuttled a little ways with his left hand clutching at his side. His right hand was stretched out in front of him, and then he swept it around and out to his side, all the while making noises as if he were in pain.

I was so overcome with pity for him, I could almost have summoned up the strength and courage to fight those monsters again right then and there. One of them almost provoked me to it when he came up to see what was going on, and looked as though he was going to hit Popcorn. But he boy finally got up, bowing submissively to the guard, and proceeded outside.

Out there, I paced back and forth; the two former prison gua sat off by themselves, and Popcorn refused any compassion timacy from Tanya now in the daylight hours, in front of o She sat by herself, and he retreated to a corner by a wall a with his back to us the whole time.

W went inside, Popcorn sat on the floor of his cell

the rest of the day with his back to the outside. One certainly couldn't blame him for spurning all human contact, when so-called humans had so successfully broken him and dehumanized him more thoroughly than the undead ever could. Ill-fed and depressed, with my whole body aching and one eye swollen shut, I myself could do nothing all day but pass in and out of sleep, sitting up in the cell, and repeating my new favorite prayer from the night before: "O Lord of hosts, that judgest righteously, let me see thy vengeance on them."

Toward evening, with deer again roasting on the fire outside, it seemed to darken early in the prison, and thunder could be heard faintly in the distance. I smirked and grunted, the only right way to register enjoyment of a dark and deadly irony. The kind of sudden, violent summer storm that swept through this time of year seemed perfect for what I thought was coming that night.

Looking over at Popcorn's battered and bruised back, I had gotten my own thousand yard stare. And it was not out of pity for the undead, as I had felt it so many times before. It was out of rage and disgust for the living. And I felt some of the raw, primal energy of outrage and revulsion that Frank had tapped into the night before.

Tonight, I would help see God's vengeance extend even here, to the deepest pit of this manmade hell. God and I had let this place be stained with innocent blood, and I blamed both of us for it. Now it was time for these walls to be painted with the blood of the guilty, the way hell was supposed to be, with righteous judgment and richly deserved, never-ending punishment.

I looked heavenward. "Give me the strength, God," I said quietly. Thunder boomed closer. I clenched my fists and could extend them without as much pain as before. I looked outside my cell and could focus a little better with my one good eye, enough to have a little bit of depth perception.

I nodded. "Thanks," I said. "That'll do."

We were again treated to the barbaric venison feast outside, though there was none of the fruit liquor this time. I was grateful not to smell its nauseating odor this night, but it meant the inmates would be sober and better able to fight us off. I guess I didn't care at this point. We all ate ravenously as storm clouds swirled above us, though as yet no rain had fallen.

When I looked at Tanya, I felt sure that I saw a look of defiance and determination. I hoped it was the same look she saw on my face. And I hoped that it would end somewhat differently for us than it had for poor Frank.

With Frank dead, and me and Popcorn beaten into bloody pulps the night before, the Pit crew didn't seem to worry about our ability to fight them off. They had two guards on Popcorn, but only one on me and Tanya, as before, with several more hanging back, ready to jump in if necessary.

With the prison now in semi-darkness, punctuated by flashes of lightning, Copperhead descended the ladder and approached Tanya's cell. He too seemed satisfied that there would be no uprising, as no bodyguard accompanied him. He even felt optimistic enough to stop and taunt me before going in to Tanya's cell.

"Big storm tonight," he said with his mock cheerfulness—though, of course, I'm sure the prospect of sadism and degradation really did make him feel cheerful. "But I'm sure you'll still hear my new black bitch screaming my name when I show

her how a real man gives her some hard lovin'. Ain't nothing gonna be loud enough to drown *that* out once I get all up in her shit." He guffawed. I prayed it would be his last.

As Copperhead baited me, another group of pedophiles entered Popcorn's cell. I made no move toward the door. Better not to raise the alarm prematurely; I felt sure that Popcorn or Tanya would attack the monsters at any moment, and that would be the signal for me to jump in and do whatever I could before they beat me to death. I still assumed it would end with my death, though I hoped to take more of these ugly bastards with me than poor Frank had.

The lightning flashed, and I only counted to five before the sound of the thunder rolled through. The storm was getting close.

I stared intently at Popcorn's cell. Both guards had gone in with the visitor this time, I assume to administer another beating if necessary. Popcorn must've timed his attack just right, though, as I heard one of them yell, "Shit! Look out! Little bastard's got a . . ."

This switched abruptly to a gurgling scream as a huge arc of red shot out between the bars to splatter on the floor outside the cell.

"Get him off me!" another man yelled. "Get him off me!" This also trailed into another horrible scream.

Neither the inmates nor I had thought Popcorn would improvise a weapon, though, in hindsight, it was hard to believe we'd overlooked the possibility. Prisoners had been turning practically anything into a weapon ever since there were prisons, and usually with much less motive than Popcorn. If a man could spend weeks making something into a knife to kill another man for a pack of cigarettes, then certainly someone fighting against torture and humiliation could be counted on to fashion something sharp and deadly.

It suddenly hit me that when he'd stumbled that morning, it was all a ploy so he could hunt around on the floor for a piece of glass big enough to do the job. And judging by the screaming, it was just the right size.

I came out the door of my cell and went for the guard. It was the same guy as I had fought the night before—an ugly, bald, squat little bastard. He came at me with the rebar and a long, rusty knife.

We both snarled as we collided. I grabbed both his hands, and we wrestled for the weapons. He tried to kick me in the groin again, but I turned slightly to the side, and it did nothing; I tried to headbutt him, but he pulled back, and I grazed his nose, to no effect.

The adrenalin and the outrage pushed me on, but he was better fed and stronger, with a lower center of gravity. Neither of us could gain the upper hand.

On the tier above us, more men came out to watch. If some of them came down to help, as they had the night before, then it would all be over just as quickly as it had been then.

But as we struggled there, Copperhead come staggering out of Tanya's cell, with her hanging onto his back and screaming like an avenging fury. I couldn't exactly see, but she was strangling him from behind, with something wrapped around his neck. I guessed it was her shoelace, something else they'd overlooked in their laziness and stupidity, and which my naiveté had been unable to identify as a potential weapon.

He couldn't grab her, and he was staggering about now, looking for someone else to hit her for him, but it wasn't working. The guard in front of her cell, who carried the baseball bat

with nails that had killed Frank, couldn't get a good shot at her, and he couldn't decide whether he should help the guy who was fighting me.

So Copperhead threw himself back against the bars of the cell, slamming Tanya into them with all his weight. I didn't think it was going to work, judging by how determined she looked. It also made it impossible for anyone else to take a swing at her.

When the crowds above saw Copperhead's predicament, they did not rush down the ladders to his aid. Instead, the same cheer as the night before rose up—"Kill! Kill! Kill!" This time it was punctuated by thunderclaps that were louder and closer each time. Clearly, the inmates were not only lacking in intelligence or a work ethic, but also in loyalty. It was hardly surprising—a place fueled exclusively on testosterone, barely-cooked red meat, sodomy, and fear would surely be lacking in those other qualities.

I suppose if Copperhead somehow came out on top, they could always claim later that they were cheering him on, so it made double sense not to get involved, but instead to enjoy the show. They regarded Copperhead fighting for his life as just an unusual and therefore very enjoyable entertainment—which, to be fair to them, was exactly how he would've regarded them in a similar situation.

This unexpected cheer also made the Pit crew hesitate. Several who had rushed to Popcorn's cell were now backing away and looking up at the crowd. Without a leader, and with its loyalties divided, the animalistic mob was much less frightening, and much less effective at either inflicting pain, or even at defending itself.

Perhaps our fight would last a bit longer than the previous night. I still assumed we would all die, but it now looked as though we had a real chance to kill Copperhead and several of the Pit crew. I could easily—no, *gladly*—accept that outcome.

Chapter Eighteen

BUT AT THE MOMENT, I was still locked in a struggle with the guard. This ended abruptly when Popcorn flew in from my right and grabbed the guy's left arm. Popcorn was snarling like a beast and was already covered in fresh, hot blood from the men he had stabbed. He climbed up on the guy I was fighting, holding onto him and biting his forearm, as he plunged a shard of glass into the guy's neck. I was showered with blood as it shot from his neck and came flying off the shard as it repeatedly slashed up and down.

The guard screamed and staggered backward. I grabbed the rebar away from him as he collapsed. He fell to his knees, with his left hand clutching at his neck, blood pouring from between his fingers. The crowd's chant of, "Kill! Kill! Kill!" crescendoed, but I hardly needed any encouragement. There could be no mercy, both for what he had done, and for what he would become if I let him bleed to death. The last thing we needed was a zombie in here.

I brought the rebar down on his head once, then again when he fell onto his face. The crowd above us let out a cheer, just as they had when Frank was being murdered last night. As

one might have expected, their cheering did not indicate approval of the winner, but merely excitement and near orgasmic joy at the maiming and killing they were witnessing.

Popcorn stood up beside me. Now his face and especially his mouth were covered with blood. It was even streaked throughout his long, wild hair. He was panting and licking his lips like a wild, rabid beast, which was not far from what he was at that moment. I couldn't say I blamed him, or even that I found the behavior all that disturbing, under the circumstances. I think anything short of drinking the blood or consuming the flesh of his tormentors would have been defensible, even decent, behavior.

I looked over, and Copperhead was still throwing himself backward against the bars of the cell, smashing Tanya into them. It didn't look fun for either of them, but she clearly seemed to be holding her own, and he seemed to be weakening.

The guy with the baseball bat finally decided to make a move toward me and Popcorn. I think at this point it was mostly an attempt to fight past us and just climb out of the Pit altogether. Good. We were no longer on the defensive, and we even had the crowd's support, if not their sympathy, for I doubt they had any. Maybe we wouldn't die that night.

The guard swung the bat at Popcorn, who nimbly jumped out of the way. He swung the bat at me, and I swung the rebar to counter it. The rebar stuck between some of the nails, so that we were then wrestling over the weapon. Popcorn dove for the guy's throat, but this time he let go of the bat to defend himself. They wrestled, and Popcorn continually slashed at his arms and throat. I disentangled the rebar from the bat and smashed the guy across the head with it once, then again, then one last time after he'd fallen. The crowd cheered wildly.

I handed the bloody rebar to Popcorn and took up the bat myself. With no more Pit crew near us, we finally ran over to help Tanya. She was wheezing and sweating from being slammed into the metal bars, but it was obvious now that she could feel the life ebbing from her tormentor. She looked at me, her teeth gritted, lips pulled back in a snarl, her eyes filled with rage, her mouth right next to his ear as his swollen, grotesque face turned blue.

He too was looking at me with his bugged-out eyes, and I imagined they were pleading, but I couldn't be sure. Perhaps worse, I'm not sure I would've cared whether or not they were. Worse still, the thought flashed through my adrenalin-soaked brain that if they were definitely pleading for mercy—something from which Frank and Popcorn had so bravely refrained—it might make what we all knew was coming next even more delectable. And I cringed, for the prospect of wreaking vengeance and punishment on this piece of filth was already terrifyingly sweet.

"You know, Jonah," Tanya hissed, "you probably don't know this, since you're not some inbred, redneck asshole who crawled out of some swamp—but you got to hit a snake in the head really hard if you want to kill its stupid, sorry ass."

I swung the bat back to deliver the blow. It was the cruel, up close and personal type of execution that a sadist like Copperhead would've found especially enjoyable, so I tried not to revel in it too much. But after the suffering of Frank and Popcorn, it was just plain impossible not to. You had to allow human nature some visceral, fleshly enjoyment from curing such a disease as Copperhead, like lancing a ripe boil, or even picking at a scab. I would've been much more inclined to show mercy to one of the undead.

Above us, the chant of, "Kill! Kill! Kill!" rose to an orgiastic crescendo.

"Die, you stupid son of a bitch." I slammed the bat into his forehead. The glitch and crunch was much louder this time than it had been with Frank, close as I was. I pulled the bat back, wrenching the nail loose from his skull, then Tanya shoved him off with a shriek of disgust as the crowd above us went wild. He fell onto his face with a thud that was barely audible above the cheers.

Tanya and I were panting, and our satisfaction was so intoxicating that we paused along with Popcorn to watch the puddle of thick, dark blood spread out from under his face. I looked at Tanya, and the bliss was almost of post-coital quality.

At that point, I really didn't care if the other inmates put my head on a stick. I'd sent the ruler of this pathetic little hell to the real thing. If anything else good ever happened to me now, or even if I just kept breathing for a few more minutes to enjoy this victory, then that was just gravy, and I'd put it on my list of things that hinted at a God interested in the guilty being punished. He had, at least, answered the prayer I had made when I buried Frank the night before.

The three of us stood there a moment, panting and covered with the warm and sticky blood, before two more screams tore through the prison, accompanied by lightning flashes and nearly immediate thunderclaps. The cheering above us stopped suddenly. The screams were long, piercing, as though from people who were being torn apart, and at the exact same moment that I heard them, I inhaled the strongest odor—even over the nearly overpowering metallic smell from all the blood—of rotting flesh. And then I could hear the other sound—a low and persistent moaning.

I really didn't want to, but I slowly turned around, away from Copperhead's body, and I saw that about forty feet away from where we stood, extending all the way back to the entrance to the prison, the ground floor was packed with swaying, shuffling human shapes. It must've finally started raining, as steam was rising off of them, as if they were soaking wet.

At the next lightning flash, I could see their rotten, undead visages—their blackened teeth, bloody mouths, foggy eyes, mottled flesh, and matted manes of straw-like hair. And though some were at present occupied with devouring two of the Pit crew, those in the vanguard were staggering toward us with their usual lack of coordination, and complete superabundance of determination and focus.

Defeating sadists and rapists only to be confronted by an army of the drooling undead—this place was about as close to hell as I hoped I would ever get. Now it seemed that we were most definitely going to die that night. It seemed it would be a lot quicker than I had previously imagined, but every bit as horrible, too.

I made sure to tack on a little extra prayer right then—that my guts were torn out and eaten before Popcorn's and Tanya's, so I wouldn't have to see that happen to them. No, wait, that would be selfish and unfair. But it didn't seem right to pray for them to die first. What the hell, I guess we could leave that part up to the Lord, as He always seemed to have the part down where innocent people died horribly, so I stopped praying and started to back up slowly.

Chapter Nineteen

In the flashes of lightning, we watched with a mixture of satisfaction and revulsion as the army of the undead took care of the two Pit crew members they had caught off guard. With a rending and a popping sound, one arm was torn from its torso, and a geyser of blood shot up after it. The two pieces were born in opposite directions in the writhing tangle of groping, eager hands. The other guy had already fallen into the crowd, and similar rending sounds could be heard as he was dispatched. Once their screams subsided, there was only a grotesque chorus of tearing and slurping.

To stem the tide of the undead, the men on the second tier pulled up the one rope ladder. Another guy had nearly reached the top of the other ladder; they pushed him off into the hungry horde, where the horrible screams and rending sounds started up again, as the inmates cut that ladder and threw it down.

As we slowly backed up, the undead reached the cell where Popcorn had been. The guy he had originally slashed lay outside on the floor. He must've still been alive, as they grabbed at him, their fingernails digging into the huge wound on his neck and tearing it wider.

He was too weak to scream, but a lightning flash made the overwhelming fear in his eyes quite apparent. Good. To be torn apart and eaten alive was indeed frightening, as I was starting to realize myself, for it seemed all too likely that it would be my fate as well. But I could still smirk at him because he had the added fear of being dragged before an angry God—for what other kind of God could possibly have created something as obscene and violent as the hungry undead?—right after beating a child nearly to death.

As more hands joined in the bloody rending, his eyes were covered, and they tore his head and his torso in two different directions, a river of blood spilling onto the floor when they finally tore the head loose, leaving behind a stump of ragged flesh.

The other Pit crew member Popcorn had slashed had staggered out, clutching at the mortal wound on his neck, blood still pouring out between his fingers and further inciting the undead's unholy hunger. Those zombies not already feeding on the headless corpse grabbed both his arms and pulled in opposite directions.

At first, it was a comical tug of war: the dead rocked him back and forth as he whimpered, too weak to muster a real scream. But when both sides finally pulled at the same time, the effect was less comical, at least for their victim, though I could still manage a cruel smile. No longer capable of fear, but just registering unspeakable pain, his eyes bugged out before both his arms tore off.

He hung there a moment, swaying slightly, mouth open, eyes rolled back in his head, blood spurting out both stumps at his shoulders with a flow that steadily weakened. Good—it seemed a more horrible version of Frank's suffering the night before.

Finally, he slumped forward and more zombies fed on his body.

I thought the undead were finished with Popcorn's tormentors at that point, but I had forgotten there was a third inmate in his cell, probably the evening's potential customer. As the undead's horrible feeding frenzy proceeded outside the cell, a weak voice came from inside, "Help! Damn kid stabbed my eyes! I can't see! Who's there? What? What? No!"

Again, the voice trailed off into screams as the undead found their blind and helpless prey. For some reason, his screams seemed to last especially long. Blinded, with claws and teeth tearing into his flesh from all sides, reducing him in seconds from a human being to a pile of meat—I hoped he spent eternity in hell like that, for what he'd done, or even just intended. I looked down at Popcorn, and he was smiling and grunting.

I guessed it was going to be the high point of our evening, for with the Pit crew devoured or retreated, and the means of getting to the second tier cut off, we were the only thing left on the menu. I clutched the bat tighter, and we kept backing up.

Chapter Twenty

I LOOKED OVER my shoulder and saw that we'd been joined by the two former prison guards, who cowered behind us. "Back into the one cell," I hissed at them. We were already almost there.

"And then what?" they blubbered.

We were backing into the cell. "And then we'll take turns at the door to the cell, killing them," I said. "They can only come at us one at a time there."

They both scuttled to the back corner of the cell. "So what? There must be hundreds of them! And you know that none of those assholes are going to come down from upstairs to help!"

I handed the bat to Tanya, and I leaned down over the two guards, my fists and face still covered in blood. "Then we'll pile up their rotted bodies ten deep till they can't get at us! And then Tanya will take the rebar and smash our heads in, so we don't become one of them! If you can't help, then just stay the hell out of our damn way! How's that for a plan?"

I went back to Tanya. "Actually, I think it'll take two to cover the door," she whispered. "These nails will get stuck—somebody else better be bashing them with the rebar at the same time."

The dead were closing slowly. "Okay," I said. "That's what

we'll do." I put my hands on Tanya and Popcorn's shoulders. "I'm sorry guys. I wish it would've turned out different."

They nodded.

Suddenly, the dead stopped, swaying and letting out a rumble of discontent or alarm. The lightning flashed again, and a ripple went through the crowd; a path opened up in it. The crowd parted, and a tall, lean figure emerged, carrying a staff.

As the thunder crashed in the darkness, we could just barely see the figure stride across the remaining yards between us and the army of the undead, and at the next lightning flash, it was right in front of us. It was Milton.

He embraced Tanya and Popcorn at the door, then pushed them farther into the cell, so he could take up a position guarding it. Now there was no way for the dead to get at us, past the leader whom they feared so much, for whatever reason.

"What's the old guy going to do?" the cowering guards bleated.

I glared at them. "Will you two just shut the hell up? Just trust us, okay?"

I patted Milton on the back, shaking my head; I couldn't believe he had the audacity to attack the prison with an army of the undead. "Thanks, Milton."

He looked over his shoulder and smiled. "You're most welcome. Where's Frank?"

I shook my head. "He didn't make it. They killed him."

Milton looked shocked and suddenly began shaking. "What—the dead I brought in here? They killed him? Oh my God!"

"No, no, not them," I said quickly, trying to calm him down. "The guys who run this place. They killed Frank last night."

"Oh, I'm so sorry. But I couldn't have lived with myself

if it was because of me." He calmed down just a little bit in the pause. "But why would they do such a thing?"

With walking corpses shuffling around in front of him, sniffing at him and eager to tear the flesh from our bones, it was really quite extraordinary to see that the regular, human evil we had all lived with our whole lives could still so shock and astonish Milton. "Frank was trying to protect Popcorn," I said. "They wanted to . . . you know . . . they wanted to hurt him . . . like that."

Milton's eyes went wide, and I could see he was fighting back tears, trying not to look weak in front of Popcorn, let alone show him pity to his face. "Good God . . . But he's only a child. I'm sorry, I had no idea there was still such evil in the world. I thought we'd been through enough."

His eyes turned to rage, for the only time I'd ever seen, and he leaned farther out the door. "I brought these maggot-ridden corpses in here, you bastards! Hundreds of them! And they haven't eaten in months! And now they're going to tear you all apart and send you to hell, you sons of bitches!"

I patted his back. "Easy, Milton. We'd all like to see that, but what exactly are we going to do now?"

"I'm not sure," he admitted. "I think Jack has a plan."

Just then we could see that the inmates were finally mounting some kind of counterattack. Arrows started raining down from the second tier onto the undead. But arrows, as effective as they were against living deer and humans, were one of the least effective weapons against zombies. There were various roars of protest as the arrows lodged into torsos, limbs, and necks, but you could see that almost none of those they hit were falling down. I worried, however, that one of the arrows—either stray or intended—would hit Milton.

I grabbed the mattress off the floor and shoved it in front of him. "Here, hold this in front of you in case one of those arrows comes your way!"

He turned his face away from it. "Good Lord," he choked. "It smells worse than me!"

I smiled. "That's why you're here to rescue us."

He looked over his shoulder at me, one arm stretched across the doorway, the other hugging the stinking mattress to his chest. "On my belt," he said, "there's a radio. Get it. Call Jack."

I got the walkie-talkie. "Jack?" I said into it.

"Great to hear you!" came the reply. "Sorry I got you into this. Everybody okay?"

"The prisoners killed Frank last night," I replied.

There was a pause. "That's too bad. He'd been through so much." There was another pause, and then he was all business again. "Where are you all in the building? We need to get you out."

"We're on the bottom floor, at the end farthest from the entrance. Milton is the only thing keeping us from getting eaten right now."

"Milton's got them held back for the time being?"

"Yes. But we're taking fire from the upper floors."

"That I can help with. Franny?"

"Almost there, Jack," I heard her reply.

"Our guys are on the first floor, so aim for the second," Jack told her.

"Roger that. Second floor's the target."

Over the sound of thunder, I could hear the thumping of the helicopter. It got louder and louder, then held steady. The skylights exploded with a flash, and glass and metal cascaded onto the dead outside the cell. A moment later, I could see

another flash at the smashed skylight, and with a whoosh, one of the cells on the second floor exploded amidst screams.

It must've been more of Jack's AT4s, being fired by someone now on the roof. As he had predicted, their real value would be proved should we ever have to fight the evil living, rather than the mindless dead.

With a flash and a whoosh, another cell exploded in flames and flying debris. Most of the upper cell block was now shrouded in a pall of dust and smoke as the groans of the injured drifted down to us.

No more arrows were raining down, so Milton lowered the mattress. "Glad I don't have to hold that anymore." He raised his hands up and shooed away some of the closer undead.

"Jack, we're not under fire anymore," I said into the radio, "but we're still trapped in here with no way out."

"Okay," he said. "I'm outside. You've got to describe the interior layout of the building to me, as best you can."

I tried to give him enough information for him to visualize the inside of the building, and where we were in it. Finally, he seemed satisfied. "Okay, there's a big wall in front of you, to your left?"

"That's right," I said.

"Then shield yourself from it, if you can, 'cause there's going to be a big hole in it in a few seconds."

"Okay, Jack." I lowered the radio. "Milton, cover yourself with the mattress again, as much as possible. Jack's going to blow some more things up."

"Well, all right," he winced as he raised the mattress again and turned his face away from it. "He does so like to do that, doesn't he?"

A second later, the wall just beyond Milton exploded with a roar that seemed ten times louder than when the rockets had hit on the second level. My ears were ringing like crazy this time. The zombies closest to the hole were thoroughly shredded by the blast, while those behind them were thrown back into the crowd, mangled and torn from the flying debris. There was now a path from the door of the cell to the hole in the wall, and we needed to go through it—fast.

I was right at Milton's back. "You okay?" I asked. He coughed slightly and nodded.

Jack and one of his men came through the hole, firing pistols. Headlights were shining through the hole as well. Jack spotted us. "Come on!" he shouted, as the dead regrouped and began pressing toward him, tripping over the body parts and corpses of their fallen comrades.

I shoved Milton forward and told him to hold back the zombies. Then I hustled the others out of the cell. "Run toward Jack!" I shouted.

They made it through the hole in the outside wall, and I was following them when a hand grabbed my ankle and tripped me up.

"No!" Milton shouted, and he slammed his staff down on the undead wrist. Its hold wouldn't break, and it was pulling its maw up to my ankle. But with a second blow, Milton severed the arm at the rotted wrist. I got up and dashed through the hole with the bony appendage still attached to my ankle. Jack and his partner were right behind me, leaving Milton to prevent his former army from coming through the hole after us.

Once outside, I kicked at the undead hand until I finally got it off of me. The small dump truck was parked thirty feet from the hole in the wall, and we all climbed into the back of it,

while Jack got in the driver's seat. He pulled the truck right up next to Milton and opened the door. Milton turned and jumped in as Jack tore off, with dead hands grasping at the side of the vehicle.

As we drove off, the helicopter rose from the roof of the prison and headed toward the museum.

A few raindrops hit us in the back of the dump truck, but the storm was passing to the south and east. The stars were coming out above us now, and the moon was half hidden by the retreating clouds. The rain had cooled everything, and the air had the freshness that it has after a cleansing storm. It was especially pronounced after the stale and rancid air of the prison, and the reek of the undead.

I looked up and breathed in deeply, and almost in spite of myself muttered, "Thanks, God. Really, this time."

Four of us had gone into hell, and three had come out. We were hardly unscathed, but we had survived. In the world of the undead, this was as close to victory as one dared hope for.

As we drove through the gate in the razor wire fence, I could feel the truck stop. I jumped down to see what was going on.

Jack and Milton got out of the truck. Milton walked over to the gate and closed it. Then he threaded the chain that had locked it back through the gate and the fence. "Jack, do you have something to hold this with?" he asked.

Jack slapped his pockets, the way people do when they're trying to see if they have the exact change or something. "You mean people-proof, or zombie-proof?" he asked.

"Just enough to hold it for a while, if some zombies come sniffing around and press up against it." Jack fumbled around in the cab of the truck for a minute. He came back with the key ring from off the truck's ignition key.

"Will this do?"

"Perfect." Milton put it through two links of the chain holding the gate closed.

"What are you doing, Milton?" I finally asked.

"I think he wants to make sure they're stuck in there with his zombie army for a while," Jack replied. "Until they're all eaten." Almost on cue, screams and gunfire could be heard, coming from the prison.

"More than that," Milton said in his dreamy sort of way. "When I was herding the zombies into here, I began to think, why couldn't I just herd all of them in here? It would be perfect, a place to keep them, so they couldn't bother the living anymore, and we wouldn't have to kill them."

I shook my head. "Milton, there are several billion of those things wandering around on the earth now. The most you could push around in front of yourself with a staff would be a dozen or so. I assume you only got so many into the prison tonight because they were all bunched up at the gate."

Milton smiled back and shook his head. "Now don't jump so far ahead, Jonah. Just because there are too many in the world is no excuse for me not to round up the ones I can, to protect you all living at the museum, and make your lives easier and safer. I realized as I led this army in there, against those evil men, that it had been wrong of me to fight against the dead, once I learned they couldn't hurt me. I should've been trying to help them."

Jack laughed. "*Help* them? Now you really are just talking

crazy, Milton. Get back in the truck and let's get back to the museum."

"No, it's a beautiful night now," Milton said wistfully. "I'm going to round up a few of our dead brothers and sisters, and put them in their new home, away from you all, and where they can do some good, punishing and eliminating the evil living, and turning them into docile, calm dead. You'll see how well it works out."

Jack knew that arguing with Milton was usually pointless. He knew Milton couldn't be hurt by the undead, so letting him wander around outside the museum with a new project wasn't that bad of an idea. "Well, Milton, okay," he said. "You know where to find us. Stop by when you need food or supplies. Give him back the radio," Jack said to me, and I handed it to Milton.

"You know I will, Jack," Milton said. "I'll come back to see you all, and to see my beloved books, that helped me so much. And you'll excuse me if I don't round up the dead too much in the winter. But I have a few months before that, to help you out." Milton turned toward me. "I am so sorry that you all suffered so much in there, and that Frank is gone. Be good to one another and heal your pains. And I'm sorry I misinterpreted your name, way back when we first meant."

"I don't understand," I said.

"Cain slew his brother, as we all have now in this undead world, and that was all that you and I remembered about him. But I was rereading the story again, last night. I was looking for some guidance as I prepared to come into battle to save you all, and for some reason I turned there. And I saw I had forgotten that Cain also built the first city. Help build our city, Jonah, the right way. You've been in the belly of the beast—thank God for less than three days, but I think long enough to see how bad the city of man can become." He gestured back toward the prison.

I nodded. "Yes, Milton, I have. And yes, I want to help build our city."

He smiled and leaned close. "And one day, when I'm too old and tired to be rounding up the dead, I hope you'll let me take some people to a meadow I know, where there's plenty of fresh water and green grass, and we can live there and pick strawberries, and grow old in peace." I hugged him like the friend and mentor he had become to me.

He stepped back and turned to address everyone. "You will all see me again," he said. "This is not goodbye. Our friends' suffering, and the destruction of this terrible, evil place have made me see a new way! Together we will grow and live, like we never dreamed we ever could again! Finally, there will be more living, and less dying!" He waved to us, then turned and wandered off the road, into the moonlit fields, whistling a little tune.

The rest of us returned to the museum, where we wept for poor Frank, and for all the horrors we had seen, until we all dozed off finally, shortly before dawn.

Epilogue

Milton's idea turned out to be his best ever, by far. Within days, we saw the zombie population near the museum drop to where we could come and go much more safely, barely having to set up distractions. Within weeks, they were seldom seen anywhere near the museum.

Milton got so good at rounding them up that we had to clear the barricade from the other end of the bridge to allow him freer access to herd them across the river and out to the prison. It was good to see the barricade go, for it made us feel we were less under siege and could live a more normal—if still difficult and dangerous—existence.

I was so gladdened by the barricade being moved that I talked Jack into taking one of the small sculptures from the museum grounds and setting it up on the site, with a makeshift plaque, to commemorate the battle there. The war with the undead would have its own Gettysburgs and Normandys, and we would honor those who fought. We could even now afford to honor and respect the dead, rather than just cower in fear behind walls from them. Most of all, we could feel that this war would have the one thing that all wars were supposed to have,

but which we had long since lost all hope of seeing—an end.

Jack began plans on extending the museum's walls to include the park across the street and some other nearby buildings. He had found a building site with plenty of supplies and began hauling them back to the museum. The park would be a special prize, as it would dramatically increase the amount of farmland for next year. And the farming this year was successful enough. By the fall, we were eating fresh fruits and vegetables every day, though we still didn't have enough to set aside for winter, nor did we have the equipment necessary for preserving them.

My experience in the prison had convinced me to talk the museum people into doing some hunting in the nearby countryside; we deserved to have some benefit from our brief and violent association with those carnivorous monsters. On one of these raids into the countryside, someone thought to grab some small farm animals, and we began to look more actively for them, acquiring a small number of chickens and goats, with plans for more once we had the space.

With material prosperity improving in the compound, Jack and I would gaze across the river and dream of the day we'd reclaim the city completely. "Looks like we're getting close to taking that rowboat out on the river, Jonah," he would kid me, "and do some fishing, like we planned."

The emotional and personal lives within the compound had kept pace with the material improvements as well. Sarah and Jack had, for all intents and purposes, adopted Zoey. Among the luggage Frank had brought, they found some few pictures of Frank and his wife, and they kept these to show Zoey when she grew up. She was the child of two very brave people, and she should know the pride and responsibility that came with such parentage.

One day, shortly after our ordeal in the prison, I found Tanya sitting on the grass, painting her toenails. "You and Milton seemed to get such a freak on about this stuff," she said coyly to me, "that I thought I should finally humor you all, before the damn bottle dries out." She grinned up at me. She almost giggled, and once you met Tanya—at least as I had known her in a world of the living dead—you knew giggling was not part of her behavior.

I sat next to her. "They look good," I said. "I knew they would. What are you so happy about?"

She put her arm around me and leaned close. "Oh, it's pretty normal, I think: happiest times in a gal's life are usually when she learns she's pregnant." And, allowing for all the irregularities of our situation, it was one of the happiest times of my life, too.

Soon after, we learned that Jack and Sarah were also expecting a baby. I had always thought the idea of pregnant women "glowing" was more or less concocted to distract them from the weight gain and nausea, but I had to admit that in Sarah's case, it was completely accurate. She was as radiant and joyful as a person could be.

Jack's reaction was harder to gauge. I could only suppose he had either seen the logic of procreating; either that, or the logical, foreseeable, and inevitable outcome of sex had simply caught up with him, and he just accepted it. It was impossible for me to tell with him, given his ever-joking manner about personal matters and feelings. But either way, they were both happy with having a future, and things to worry about other than shooting zombies in the head and consuming enough calories from canned food to stay alive.

And if we saw less of "our dead brothers and sisters," as

Milton now liked to call them, we hardly saw any less of him. If anything, his constant sojourns to round up the dead and put them in their new home seemed to cure him mostly of his illness, so he had more energy and was in less pain.

Those of us without his affliction whispered darkly that it seemed like a terrible price to pay—having to walk among the reeking, rotting dead in order to feel more alive—and it seemed to bespeak a frightening, shameful kinship between Milton and his dead brothers and sisters, but there was no denying that it benefited all of us immensely. So even though Milton slept every other night out in the countryside somewhere between the museum and the prison, we saw him nearly as often as we used to, and he was always in the highest of spirits.

I remember one time, in the early fall, when the weather was about like it had been when I had first arrived at the museum—a glorious, clear, warm, almost painfully bright day. But in the fall, such a day would always hold the threat of cold and death to come, rather than the springtime's promise of rebirth and life and growth. But this day, such thoughts did not really make us sad, so much as they made us merely thoughtful and introspective, like Milton always was, regardless of the weather. Jack, Tanya, Sarah, and I were out on the roof of the museum, watching Milton move a particularly large mob of the dead. He had with him two dogs that he had found on his trips, and which had become instantly devoted and loving, while he had likewise become instantly enamored of their simple loyalty and good sense. He now used the dogs to help him herd the dead, so that he could now handle hordes over a hundred.

"It's so damned weird, watching him herd them," Jack said.

"I think it's cute," Sarah said. Unlike Tanya, giggling came quite naturally to her.

"It's still weird," Jack continued. "He looks like he's their shepherd. It's as if they like him or something. I don't know if that's right."

"He looks like a damn zombie Jesus," Tanya added. We all turned to stare at her. She was right, of course, but it still sounded strange, almost taboo, even if you weren't religious. "Well, he *does*," she insisted. "I mean, I don't remember Jesus having any dogs, but you got to admit—it's what he looks like. But maybe it's how it's supposed to be. Jesus was part man and part God, so he could save man. Milton's part man and part *them*—no offense to him, you understand—so he can save them. And us."

Tanya was, as usual, quite right. We had our messiah, and so did the dead. We had our little community. We had our love and our children. And as hard as the past year had been, there was nothing more that we could legitimately ask for, and nothing more for which to blame God. We had been tried in a way more horrible than any of us could've imagined, but we had survived when none of us would've guessed it possible. Jack's million little coincidences and lucky breaks had all come together in such a way that the gates of hell—quite literally—had not prevailed against us.

Acknowledgments

THE PERSON WHO has read and commented the most on the manuscript is Robert P. Kennedy, with great enthusiasm and encouragement for my new project. At the same time, W. Scott Field—with his extensive knowledge of things military—has provided frequent and enormous assistance about the fine points of modern weapons systems, explosives, and tactics. William Lebeda's comments have been of a more aesthetic and less technical nature, but he too has been a constant inspiration to me to pursue my writing in this genre. Marylu Hill, as the token non-horror person among my initial readers, has often provided the outsider's perspective that helps keep my writing from becoming too narrow or constrained by its genre. Finally, my editors at Permuted Press—Jacob Kier and D.L. Snell—gave the manuscript its final tweaking and tightened up a lot of loose points.

The city in the story is based very loosely on Grand Rapids, Michigan, where I spent two recent summers studying at Calvin College as part of the Seminars in Christian Scholarship (see http://www.calvin.edu/scs). I saw no point in naming it explicitly in the story, as the factor of local color would not carry the kind of weight it does with more famous locales, and I would then be endlessly criticized for any necessary departures from the details of the real-life city. For maps and description of local landmarks like the Van Andel Museum, see http://www.visitgrandrapids.org.

People are always curious about one's literary influences. I don't think most of my exemplars are typical of horror writers, but I suspect that what we think of as "typical" is an unfair generalization, and horror writers are as diverse in their tastes as doctors, lawyers, or college professors. However, the influence of—and even direct allusions to—several books that have haunted me for decades are scattered throughout the present work. Alert readers will readily spot images taken from Dante's *Inferno*, Melville's *Moby-Dick*, several of Shakespeare's plays, and, of course, the Bible. What work of literature could be truly horrifying without drawing on the accumulated depictions of evil throughout Western literature?

But beyond details or allusions, I would have to say many of the ideas in this book ultimately go back to two men whose works I first encountered about a quarter century ago. First, St. Augustine, for his most profound and influential ruminations on human depravity that still, to this day, fifteen centuries after he lived, do not merely influence discussions of sin and evil, they more or less determine what will be discussed, the terms in which the concepts can be discussed, and, to a large extent, the conclusions that can be drawn.

And second, of course, no zombie book or film today can fail to acknowledge George A. Romero, for completely determining the identity, meaning, and importance of zombies in our culture. Influences from and allusions to his films abound in the present work, as they must in any zombie film or fiction today. I believe the continuing ability of Romero's zombie hordes both to scare and challenge us in our arrogance makes them as potent and relevant as St. Augustine's more overtly theological work. They continue to have "bite," as it were.

Finally, thanks are always due to my family, during and after any writing project. My obsession with monsters is tolerated by my wife, Marlis, and our daughter, Sophia, while it is enthusiastically encouraged by our son, Charles.

Kim Paffenroth
Cornwall on Hudson, NY
June 2010